Mary Dunn
a noted pr
contribut
London
famous c
Addle. She was
historian Andrew Shirley
daughter by him. She died in 19

Also by Mary Dunn

LADY ADDLE REMEMBERS

and published by Black Swan

The World of Lady Addle

THE MEMOIRS OF MIPSIE

Mary Dunn

With an Introduction by
Simon Hoggart

BLACK SWAN

The World of Lady Addle
THE MEMOIRS OF MIPSIE
A BLACK SWAN BOOK 0 552 99192 9

Originally published in Great Britain by Robin Clark Limited in conjunction with Punch Publications

PRINTING HISTORY
Robin Clark/Punch edition published 1985
Black Swan edition published 1986

Most of the material in *The Memoirs of Mipsie* appeared originally in *Punch,* and is reprinted by kind permission of the Proprietors.

Corgi Books are published by Transworld Publishers Ltd., 61-63 Uxbridge Road, Ealing, London W5 5SA, in Australia by Transworld Publishers (Aust.) Pty. Ltd., 26 Harley Crescent, Condell Park, NSW 2200, and in New Zealand by Transworld Publishers (N.Z.) Ltd., Cnr. Moselle and Waipareira Avenues, Henderson, Auckland.

Made and printed in Great Britain by the Guernsey Press Co. Ltd., Guernsey, Channel Islands.

INTRODUCTION
by Simon Hoggart

Mary Dunn was born in 1900, the youngest of three children. Her father was Arthur Dunn, in his day a considerable sporting celebrity who even played soccer for England. His life story is wonderfully evocative of an age which exists now only in rather improbable fiction, such as that which his daughter wrote. Certainly the attitudes he held and the social world in which he moved must have provided much of the background she used.

Dunn played for Old Etonians in the year they won the FA Cup, 1882, and he laid on the only goal of the match through wizard dribbling down the wing. Mary Dunn later recorded that this had come as a severe shock to the Etonians' opponents, Blackburn Rovers, who had invented what must be the most unlikely terrace chant ever heard in an English ground:

> All hail, ye gallant Rover lads,
> Etonians thought ye were but cads.

Sir Shane Leslie wrote a memoir of him in 1937 in which he said: 'Arthur Dunn taught us to play football as honourably as the game of life, to recite the Kings of Judah and Israel, to love God and to hate Harrow.' Mary added: 'It is possible that life for my father was as simple as that. He was untroubled by religious or philosophical doubts, and would have preferred fixing up coat hooks in the boys' changing-room to any discussion on abstract problems.' He did seem to have been remarkably obsessed by sport, to the exclusion of much else. Sir Shane noted: 'Novel reading in an armchair was his synonym for what was rank and rotten in behaviour.'

He was also an esteemed singer, partly because of the odd fact that his voice did not break while he was at school so that he was able to sing treble until the day he left. Sir Shane records:

> . . . he could have made song his life's work, but was content to give friends a very occasional reminder of his divine gift. In later days I was present at a concert of the conventional type which seldom cheers and never intoxicates. At the last moment someone called on Arthur to sing 'Tom Bowling'. Instead of applause there was dead silence, for the audience was in tears. His voice never broke, but passed from a boy's to a man's.

This event could have appeared almost verbatim in the Lady Addle books – though as it happens Mary also had a good voice and sang briefly with the D'Oyly Carte.

Dunn earned his living as headmaster of a preparatory school he had founded near Cockfosters, called Ludgrove. It still exists, though it has since moved to Wokingham. He married Helen Malcomson, the daughter of a Scottish neighbour, who at first insisted that the wedding could not take place until the school had financial security with ten boys enrolled. He relented at the ninth. Money always seems to have been fairly tight for the family, though there were several upper-class connections of the sort even a penurious Old Etonian might be expected to have. One of the Ludgrove masters became tutor to the Prince of Wales, and one of Mary's godparents was Lady Strathmore, the mother of the present Queen Mother. As a child Mary was taken for tea at Glamis Castle.

Her life seems to have been spent largely in the no-man's-land between the rich and powerful and the genteel middle classes. She married Andrew Shirley, the younger son of the Earl Ferrers, one of whose ancestors was the last peer to be hanged by a silken rope. They too never became wealthy. Andrew could not expect to inherit, and made much of his living as an art historian – in his day he was the acknowledged authority on Constable. It was his second marriage; he had formed an unfortunate misalliance while at Oxford.

The couple went to live at Royal Avenue, Chelsea, in a building which is now a supermarket. It was here that Jane, their only child, was born. They had two servants, a Swiss nannie and a sort of butler who did various jobs. Both of them complained that they could not sleep because of the other's habit of tramping about at night. One evening while they were both out the tramping continued as before, and a clairvoyant was called in to deal with the problem. She announced that the house was haunted by an old man who was guarding it. The spectre was permitted to stay, unlike the manservant, who was sacked, according to family legend, when he was caught wearing one of Andrew's Old Wykehamist ties.

At this stage in their lives Mary had begun her writing career and produced the first of the four *Lady Addle* books. They are by far the funniest work she ever did. Much of her writing was fairly bland, undemanding humour which you might wearily leaf through in a waiting-room. Lady Addle, however, was almost always sharp and cutting.

All the characters, for example, are consumed by their own complacency and self-importance. Secure in their supremacy they know that nothing is too much trouble for other people. Lady Addle thinks of her mother as a saint, for when the girls get scarlet fever, 'she insisted on our nannie remaining with us, night and day for a week, without a second's relaxing of her vigilance'. The family fox terrier becomes old and bad-tempered, so regretfully 'he had to be given to the head groom's children, as he was considered no longer safe to keep'. The premise behind *The Memoirs of Mipsie* is that the British aristocracy can do nothing wrong, pretty well by definition. Mipsie, Lady Addle's sister, is a splendid comic creation. She is variously a thief, a swindler, a fraud, a brothel keeper and a promiscuous adventuress who will do anything to get her hands on jewellery and cash. Lady Addle doesn't excuse her behaviour; it never crosses her mind that there is anything to excuse. Mipsie is an English gentlewoman, and therefore beyond the possibility of reproach.

One of the puzzles about Mary Dunn is that she combined this relish for savage attacks on the upper classes with a considerable and rather snobbish respect for them and their ways. According to Jane, her daughter, she hated hypocrisy and pretension. Yet when Jane said that she wanted to marry Ian Ross, an advertising man, both Mary and Andrew made it clear that they strongly disapproved. It was not, they explained, that they had anything personal against Ian – merely that they hoped for someone with money or a title or, with any luck, both.

When it became clear that the marriage would go ahead anyway, Ian was taken to lunch with Lady Burnham, a family friend on whose estate the Shirleys now lived. 'I was taken to Hall Barn as exhibit "A",' he recalls. 'Afterwards I made the social mistake of sending a thank-you letter. Mary was horrified and told Jane, "you much tell Ian *not* to thank for lunch".' Lady Burnham, however, was very pleased.

Mary and Andrew had moved to the country in 1937, renting Park Hill cottage – actually two cottages knocked together – on the Burnham estate near Beaconsfield. They paid £5 a week, which was a modest rent even then, especially as Mary could often cover much of the amount with an article or a comic poem for *Punch*. *Lady Addle Remembers* had gone through three editions, and its success had made her something of a local celebrity. She liked dressing up, and when Jane held garden fêtes for Dr Barnardo's her mother would open them dressed as 'Lady Park Hill', a role close to her fictional character.

The first *Lady Addle* book was published in 1936, though it was another eight years before she reappeared, this time as a weekly series in *Punch*. *Lady Addle at Home* started its run in the magazine in March 1944, under the title *Lady Addle's Domestic Front*. The war was almost over, and there is an optimistic light-heartedness about the magazine: a political cartoon shows Stalin mounted on a bulldozer, clearing away Nazi rubble. A young housewife asks: 'How would you like your egg this month, dear?'

It is remarkable how many of the people who appeared then are still writing today. Basil Boothroyd, Humphrey Ellis (who wrote the A.J. Wentworth BA books), Richard Price and Paul Jennings were in these issues; David Langdon and J.W. Taylor still draw cartoons. In his history of *Punch*, written in 1957, Richard Price gave one of the very few contemporary written judgements on Mary Dunn:

> She started from the same kind of jumping-off point as several of the rather indistinguishable band of feminine contributors who localized a substantial proportion of *Punch*'s pages in Kensington; but her humour was bludgeoning and destructive, her effects broader. Her most famous series, the mock memoirs of a character called 'Lady Addle' produced rather strained smiles but gave much pleasure to the irreverent. It was cheerful, hit-or-miss fun, and the tone was loud. It made one conscious of how hushed and cloistered the tone in other parts of the paper had become. Lady Addle behaved as no peeress in Angela Thirkell would have behaved, and her creator was allowed an occasional innuendo that it was perhaps assumed would be omitted by Companions reading the articles aloud.

In *Mipsie* at least, the innuendoes are hardly occasional – they occur in almost every chapter and are spelled out with such detail that their excision must have presented Companions with a constant and worrying task.

Lady Addle's Domestic Front must have been thought a success and *The Memoirs of Mipsie* began in February 1945. Mary was paid nine guineas for each article, which seems to have been a decent if not munificent rate. The editor, E.V. Knox, was not one of those who are open-handed with his proprietor's money. People beginning their writing careers, such as A.A. Milne, were told that there would be no fee; it was honour enough to appear in *Punch*. Nor did Knox like to meet his contributors, fearing that personal acquaintance might colour his judgement. Humphrey Ellis, who was his deputy, remembers: 'When it was announced that Mr Someone-or-other had called, Knox might say: 'What *can* the man want?', though the caller had been a contributor for up to ten years.'

Both serializations were published soon afterwards as books, though without the same success as *Lady Addle Remembers* – possibly because aficionados had already read them in the magazine. The last pieces were published as *Round the Year with Lady Addle*, but by this time the humour was less easy. Mary Dunn's skill at taking an ordinary, even banal situation, then suddenly giving it a mad surrealist spin had begun to fade. She did however turn out another good series for *Punch*, called *Shattered Illusions*. On the left-hand side of the page was a set of clichéd incidents in a familiar fictional setting: the artist's garret, the diva's dressing-room, the blacksmith's at Gretna Green. On the right were the same incidents as they might happen in real life. The jokes and parody have the same bite as *Lady Addle*.

The main source for her family of appalling aristocrats must have been that kind of self-serving memoir by a lady of quality which filled many a library shelf then and can still be found today in the older London clubs and second-hand bookshops. Jane thinks that another fund of ideas might have been two of Mary's cousins on her mother's side who lived together in a state of constant social guerrilla warfare. They would bicker endlessly over such questions as which sherry glasses to use.

Though they lived in the same house, they refused to use the same headed notepaper: one spelled the address 'Wealdacre' and the other 'Weald Acre'. They used to dress expensively but in poor taste, and, dowdily attired, would appear at the annual Eton and Winchester cricket match. Jane recalls that her mother was in a state of some anxiety each year until she had tracked the cousins down and paid the necessary courtesies.

They may well have been the inspiration for the terrible social jockeying which appears throughout the books, and Jane believes that they were certainly the source of the bitchy exchange of letters between Lady Addle and her mother-in-law in *Lady Addle Remembers.*

Mary got her pictures from country-house sales, where she would buy boxes and albums full of old family photographs. These were then altered by the publishers, Methuen. Mipsie, whose sister constantly describes her as 'beautiful', is almost always decorated with hideous buck teeth. Again, the ambiguity of Mary's attitude to the nobbish classes emerged: Jane recalls her mother spreading the pictures all over the floor and giggling with pleasure at some particularly grotesque or pompous pose. Then she would say how she hoped that nobody would recognize themselves and so have their feelings hurt.

But Mary's own life rarely brought her close to the likes of Lady Addle. The Shirleys were thought a slightly raffish couple in the London of the thirties and fourties; half Bohemian, half conventional. Mary was invariably dressed smartly if somewhat eccentrically and she favoured lavish wide-brimmed hats. The late Norah Smallwood, who worked with her at Chatto and Windus when Mary was editing a series of brisk career books for girls, said: 'She was quite unflappable. She kept her poise whatever was going on around her. She always seemed to look slightly official, as if she were a lady mayoress about to open a fête.'

One of Jane's friends was Gabrielle Drew, who recalls staying at Park Hill Cottage and being taught how to make mayonnaise, then a rather exotic substance. The Shirleys always served exceedingly generous drinks to their guests, and on this occasion a lot of sherry had been consumed. At one point in the culinary siminar Gabrielle collapsed backwards into a bath. Mary carried on as if nothing had happened.

Hugh Bredin was courting Gabrielle around this time, and used to call in at the flat she shared with Jane Shirley. 'Mary seemed to me at the time a rather buttoned-up person. She would arrive at the flat every six weeks or so, and she usually seemed to have an excuse for not giving the girls advance notice.'

These unannounced arrivals were probably intended to check on the state of the flat, which belonged to Andrew and Mary and was full of excellent furniture – 'highly incompatible', Jane says, 'with a teenage lifestyle'.

Not that Mary was straight-laced. She had told Jane the facts of life and birth control before turning her loose in London – possibly as a reaction to her own mother, Helen, who was both repressive and possessive. She had expected Mary to be home well before midnight every night, even when she was in her twenties. Occasionally Mary dutifully returned, kissed her mother goodnight, then crept out back to whichever party she had left. Years later she told Norah Smallwood that she had given Jane the facts-of-life talk, and this was thought very bold and progressive.

On the other hand, Mary could be equally conventional. Hugh Bredin recalls meeting the Shirleys shortly after they had been to see *Waiting for Godot*, presumably in its first London production. 'They were fulminating that it was all part of some terrible conspiracy to take over Art. Andrew was militantly conservative in these matters, and everything he said was vociferously echoed by Mary.'

Later Bredin met Mary again, and found her light, bubbly and fun – a surprising contrast to the *grand dame* he had encountered earlier. Most people found that she could be sparkling company, when she wanted to be. She wasn't exactly witty, but she did have the knack of giving a humorous cast to any event, however workaday and dull.

The film critic Dilys Powell knew her fairly well: 'She was good-looking though not beautiful, very confident and socially poised. In those days there seemed to be a floating population in London of people who managed to make a living by writing, but who weren't really famous. She was great fun in an impudent kind of way – and she dominated her husband.'

Most of her surviving friends recall this domination, though it's fair to say that's not Jane's memory. At home the relationship was one between equals.

By the fifties she was established as a children's writer. She produced a number of travel books using Jane as the central character, made children's programmes for the BBC, and organized the children's section in book exhibitions. In 1958, Jane made it clear that she intended to marry Ian Ross in spite of her parents' high aspirations. They gave way quickly, with good grace. Jane is still happily married and works as a successful interior decorator. Ian left advertising and now runs the charity International Christian Relief.

Just before the wedding, in 1958, Mary suffered a serious attack of hepatitis and was in hospital during the ceremony. She sent a cheerful telegram signed 'From Your Chrome-Yellow Mummy' and, to Ian's embarrassment, the guests responded by singing 'For She's a Jolly Good Fellow'. A week later she died.

Andrew, miserable with grief and suffering from throat cancer, did not last the year. Jane, who thought of her mother as her best friend, felt angry and horribly cheated.

The Bookseller devoted a full page obituary to her: 'Her keenness was infectious, her energy as prodigious as her versatility, and her direct, practical approach to every problem so inspiriting that difficulties resolved themselves and one found oneself carried away on a tide of mutual enthusiasm.' The writer thought she would be best remembered for her work on children's literature. Lady Addle, after a gap of a dozen years, had been forgotten.

So, outside the family circle, had Mary herself. Dilys Powell says: 'The Shirleys just seemed to vanish from our lives. They would come to dinner, you'd meet them at parties, and suddenly they simply weren't there.'

The rest of the world forgot too, apart from a few people who found copies of *Lady Addle Remembers*, maybe sitting on a dusty shelf during a wet weekend in the country. Then, in 1983, Robin Clark republished the book to a few, but highly enthusiastic reviews. The BBC serialized it on Radio 4 in the autumn of 1984, and the book appeared in the best-seller lists, probably for the first time. Lady Addle, like her own terrible family and the whole of the British aristocracy, had proved indestructible.

The World of Lady Addle

THE MEMOIRS OF MIPSIE

MIPSIE ON HER RELEASE FROM PRISON

TO

MY HUSBAND

AN EARLY ADMIRER OF MIPSIE'S

CONTENTS

ILLUSTRATIONS

FOREWORD

By Rear-Admiral The Lord Doomsday, K.C.B., C.M.G.

It gives me great pleasure to be able to accede to the request of one of my oldest friends, Lady Addle of Eigg, to write a foreword to her memoirs of her remarkable sister. The authoress has a ready pen, and portrays delightfully many incidents and personalities of the good old days, now unfortunately long past, when men were men and women's clothes weren't the wide open spaces they seem to be nowadays. Besides this, Lady Addle can write or discourse on any modern subject with the best, owing to her unusual intellect and insight into human nature. I believe, at heart, she is still the jolly girl she was when I first knew her.

I have known all the Coot girls since they were children, and very jolly girls they were, believe me. Mipsie was always the beauty, of course—she would make every man's eyes, and often his legs too, follow her, even in the street. My grandfather, Admiral Lord Doomsday (every Doomsday has always entered the senior service since the British Navy was created, and most of us have reached flag rank), was Mipsie's godfather, and very fond of her he was, too. He would forgive her anything. 'Fast little ship like Mipsie,' I can hear the old man say with a chuckle, 'bound not to be as steady as one of your "safety first" old tanks with a flat bottom.' At the same time he was old-fashioned enough to be distressed at her many matrimonial disasters. 'Go into dock for re-fitting as many times as you like,' he would say, 'but never change your owner.' He may have been right too. He had only one wife all his life, though I've heard my father say many a time that he wouldn't have recognized her if he'd met her. Once he came back from sea unexpectedly and found my grandmother in the drawing-room. 'What the devil are you doing here?' he roared, for he had a very fine voice. 'How dare you have the infernal cheek to appear on the bridge in my presence?' She explained who she was and he was slightly mollified. 'All right, you can stay,' he said, 'but have the goodness to keep your ugly face turned away from me while I'm in the house.' He was a singularly honest man and always called a spade a spade or a woman whatever he thought she looked at the moment.

When I first met the Coot girls I was a hot-headed youngster of seventeen—a couple of years younger than Mipsie. She took me in hand at once, for I was a bit uncouth and inexperienced in those days, I've no doubt, and I shall always be grateful to her for the things she taught me. We used to go for grand boating picnics on the beautiful lake at Coots Balder. Mipsie had the most appalling memory—she has always been very absent-minded, and many's the time I've known her start off somewhere without an escort and have to stop and pick one up—and she usually seemed to forget that she had left something or other behind at the picnic site, and of course I had to row her back to get it. Then we'd contrive somehow to get late, and often it meant a wigging when we got back from the old man—Lord Coot, who was a bit of a martinet. But I didn't fret. 'Sailors don't care,' was a motto Mipsie implanted in me early.

Soon after that I was posted to Malta and thence to India, so I lost sight of Mipsie for a good many years.

Next time I saw her was in Egypt. She looked splendid on a camel and had the Sphinx beaten to a frazzle. But she did some very rash things which used to worry me a good bit. I remember once seeing her lying in a *dahabeeyah* in broad daylight, dressed only in purple sequins, with a goat bending over her. I've no idea what she was doing. She signalled to me to look the other way, which I did of course, but the whole business worried me a lot. Not long after that she made the mistake of her life in marrying Sir Constant Standing, who was a good fellow, but never had the character to hold a girl like Mipsie. Not perhaps, as I told her at the time, when I asked her to marry me, that I should have been able to keep her either. 'My dear Doom,' she said laughing, 'I don't think even King Midas would be able to keep me.' I asked her who the chap was, never having been a literary bloke myself, and she said, 'He was a man of pure gold,' from which I conclude she meant that a very ordinary sailor fellow like me would never have a chance to win her heart, which I knew only too well.

Not that I gave up the attempt. But it always seemed to be my bad luck to be on high seas when she was between husbands and on *terra firma* when she was tied up. I think the next time I saw her was when she was Princess Ubetskoi. I was a Commodore then, and had to go out on some naval mission to Ekaterinbog. I remember Mipsie immediately sending for me and giving me tea in her 'little boudoir', which was about the size of a battleship's quarter-deck. I recollect feeling a bit nervous, as I know what sticklers some of these foreigners are if one contravenes the customs of their country. But Mipsie didn't care. 'Don't worry,' she said, 'it's an old Mipsian custom and that is much more important.' There was a dark chap there, Prince Michel, her stepson, good-looking, I suppose, in a very un-English and rotten way. When I went to her boudoir the following day I found him having tea with her, and I must confess I was pretty sore. 'Is this a Mipsian custom too?' I remember asking angrily. 'No,' she said, 'just a custom of the country.' I felt ashamed of myself then, as obviously she was only asking the chap out of duty, and she certainly wasn't the girl to shirk duty, for she asked him every day, I found out later.

There came a time when I almost won her. I shall never forget it because in one week I drew the Derby favourite in the Calcutta sweep, and that same evening Mipsie, for the first time in her life, told me she would consider marrying me. I was over the moon with excitement, as may be imagined, at the possible idea of achieving a fortune—for the Doomsdays have never had overmuch of this world's goods—and the girl I loved at the same time. I suppose that made it seem all the harder when the favourite wasn't even placed and, two days later, Mipsie told me she had reconsidered her half-promise to marry me. I think that was about the only time I had one over the eighteen, to try and drown my disappointment.

Now I must give a word to Blanche, who has written this very talented biography of her sister. She was always a clever girl, who could put her hand to anything, and since her marriage she and her husband Addle, who is one of the best fellows I ever struck, have been really good friends to me. I used to admire the plucky way in which Blanche took on, without any training, the cooking for her household during the difficult times of the last war. I have often stayed with them at Bengers in the past few years, and I always made a point of taking down all my own rations, so as not to add to Blanche's anxieties by partaking of one dish of her own cooking. So kind and hospitable is she that she would often try to press me to taste one, but after my first stay, when I thought it would have been churlish to refuse, I stuck to my guns. Addle and I used to have grand contests at billiards, till Blanche commandeered the billiard table for drying herbs on. He was never what I'd call a first-class player, but a very keen one. His great ambition is to make a break of fifty and I for one hope he will achieve this one day, for he well deserves it for his sportsmanship. Never once when I have finished a break, have I seen him show signs of annoyance at being woken up. 'Let's see, where do we stand now, Doom?' he used to say when he took up his cue once more. A real sportsman and old English gentleman, which is a rarity to-day.

I must end this foreword with a story which is characteristic of Mipsie's warm heart. When the war ended and I retired from the service I thought I would smarten myself up with a lick of paint, so went off to order myself a new suit—quite unnecessarily, as it happens, as I have a whole wardrobe of suits, some as recent as 1920. But my tailor had insisted on reserving a length of pre-war tweed for me, so I thought I may as well have the stuff made up. When completed I put it on and went to take Mipsie out to lunch. Much to my surprise though, she looked quite upset about it. 'What's wrong, old girl?' I asked her. 'Don't you like it?' Mipsie shook her head. 'It's not you,' she said. 'Not the you that I know, that has seen service all over the world and never shirked his duty yet. Please, dear Doom, don't wear it—wear your dear old suits—to please me.' Well, when a girl like Mipsie asks a fellow like me a favour like that, what can one do? But I own I was a bit flummoxed. I don't care much for clothes, but I don't like waste and never have. 'But what am I to do with the blamed things? I've only just ordered them,' I said. 'Send them to me and I'll find a good home for them,' answered Mipsie, which course I accordingly took. About a month later I arrived to fetch her for lunch and something she was wearing struck me as familiar. 'Yes,' she said, laughing, 'it's your suit, converted. Do you really think I would let any one but your best friend wear any garment of yours, Doom?' I was so flattered by that that I believe I should have proposed to her again, at the age of nearly seventy, if she had not just been married to her present husband, Sir Augustus Royster. As it was I contented myself with taking her straight to Cartier's and ordering her a naval crown in diamonds so that, as she suggested, I should nail my colours to the bust, so to speak, of what will always remain the only girl in the world for me.

DOOMSDAY, Rear-Admiral,
Conquest Magna,
Hastings.

I

A METEOR IS BORN

WHAT outward sign does the world give, I sometimes ask myself, to mark the dawn of a great event, a new vital force in its midst? How did Nature acclaim the birth of Julius Caesar, of Napoleon, Nelson—or my sister Mipsie? As regards the last-named, I like to think—for I have ever had a poet's mind—that the famous Balder pink nightingales sang a gayer roundelay that June morning, that the roses in my mother's celebrated moss-rose garden threw off their modest veils for a spell and laughed up at the sun, and that the harebells in the park—it was noted for these lovely flowers, which grew fully three inches high and were of the most beautiful harebell blue—rang a merry peal that day; a pæan of praise for Mipsie.

Indeed, I have often thought that she had something in common with those great men I have mentioned. Like Caesar, whenever she came and saw, she conquered. Like Napoleon, her material gains in Europe were immense. As for Nelson—well, he wore his sleeve pinned on his heart. Mipsie's critics used to say she wore her heart on her sleeve, so frank and impulsive was her nature. So they too have a link, after a century, as I feel sure they would have had if belonging to the same generation. I cannot imagine Mipsie being beaten by a housemaid—especially one without a reference like Emma Hamilton. But I must return to my biography.

Lady Millicent Bertha Geraldine Arabella FitzTartan

Coot, third daughter of the thirteenth Earl Coot, was born at Coots Balder on June 19th, 1871. She was, I think, the only one of us who was not held up for the hounds to sniff, and curiously enough, though love of the chase is part of her very being, and I know her seat has been praised by many competent judges, she alone of our family seems born, I sometimes think, for some softer support than the saddle. She was lovely even as a baby, apparently, with blue eyes like—as my mother said—a misty sea. I, overhearing the words, repeated them in my childish lisp, 'Mip-sea'—and the name became a bedside word in five continents.

Mipsie's godparents included one Royal sponsor—an old custom in our family—Princess Bertha of Nicht-Hinausleen, Lady Geraldine (Diney) Colquholquhoun (pronounced Con), Admiral Lord Doomsday, and dear old Sir Ludovic FitzTartan.

The latter was something of a character. His favourite hobbies were shooting bees, at which he became extremely proficient, though he never, I believe, actually hit one, and racing cockroaches. I shall never forget staying at Sporran Castle, and the thrill of seeing the fascinating little creatures scuttling away from a strong light which was switched on at the starting point of the beautiful course which Sir Ludo had specially constructed for them. All the cockroaches backs were painted different gay colours, like jockeys, and excitement ran high when his guests used to back their favourite runner. But unluckily his best stud cockroach (painted gold) escaped one day into the kitchen, and thereafter the castle became so infested that Lady FitzTartan, who had long sufferingly submitted for years to having the cockroach 'stables' at the foot of their bed, at last put her own foot down, and her husband's life's work had to be abandoned.

Sir Ludo was devoted to his godchild and spoilt her

outrageously. I remember well one time when he happened to be staying at Coots Balder, and Mipsie lost the beautiful diamond pendant which he had given her at her christening (she had been dressing up her dolls in jewels!). She appeared suddenly in the drawing-room, flung herself on her godfather's knees and confessed the disaster. He comforted her lovingly, promising to give her another pendant just like the lost treasure. Mipsie looked up at him roguishly through her wet eyelids. 'Mipsie bigger girl now—bigger diamonds,' she said. How Sir Ludo roared! But he took the hint, and the new pendant was proportionately larger to match Mipsie's five years. The strange thing was that the original jewel turned up again not long afterwards, inside a doll's leg. Those kind of lucky coincidences were always happening to Mipsie, who certainly had all the good fairies present at her christening.

And what a christening it was! I was too young to remember it but it was, I am told, one of the most brilliant functions of the season. Special trains were run to Little Balder station, which was festooned in yellow and black—the Coot colours—so that 'it was just like crawling out into a gigantic wasp's nest,' as some admirer said. In addition, there was a Pullman car to bring down dear Admiral Doomsday, who was crippled with gout, but who went everywhere in his famous bath chair shaped like a fo'c'sle. This magnificent but somewhat ungainly vehicle was engineered into the reception, and the Admiral, who was a great raconteur and a very popular figure in any gathering, sat like a Sultan, drinking champagne diluted with brandy (for he was forbidden wine by his doctors) out of a silver tankard, keeping every one in fits by his witty sallies. Suddenly, he surprised the assembled company by rising, and actually walking, though rather unsteadily, over to Mipsie, who was holding a rival court in her nurse's arms. The Admiral drew nearer—then, before any one could stop him, he seized a full bottle of champagne and crying out: 'Come, let's launch this neat little craft,' swung it over his shoulders, and crashed it down on the baby's head!

It was a terrible moment. My mother screamed, and more than one brave man fainted, I am told. But Mipsie holds a charmed life. By an incredible stroke of luck the bottle broke the nurse's arm instead, while Mipsie lay almost untouched, crowing and gurgling with delight as the champagne poured over her tiny face into her mouth. Thus, with a miracle, began the career of one of the famous beauties and outstanding personalities of our time, whose sister I am proud to be, and whose romantic and vivid life history I am privileged to write in these pages.

II

NURSERY DAYS

WE were a high spirited and happy family of children, singularly pure and unspoilt in our tastes, and with an almost austere upbringing in the midst of the splendours of Coots Balder. One wing alone was given to the nurseries. Our daily fare was unvaried—chicken and sole by turns, while no fruit but peaches and grapes was allowed on the table (except during the strawberry and raspberry season, of course) with melons and pineapples on Sundays. We wore simple plush dresses in winter and fine muslin in summer. Our petticoat ribbons followed a rigid pattern as to colour; blue in winter, pink in summer, mauve in Lent. 'I want red—I will have red!' I remember Mipsie saying once, in her lovable commanding way. That night, when the butler poured out my father's port, something stuck in the neck of the decanter. It was Mipsie's ribbons, which she had attempted to dye!

Of course she was no more blamed for that escapade, though it was priceless port, of the most up-to-date vintage that money could buy, no doubt, than she was when she stole one of King Edward VII's spats and buttoned it round her small self, saying: 'I want to know what a royal leg feels like.' Or when she used a whole bottle of a visiting duchess's French scent to put behind the ears of her pet dog, Rascal, a delightful fox terrier puppy, beloved by us all. Alas, when he grew up his temper became uncertain and he had to be given to the head groom's children, as he was considered no longer safe to keep.

What a happy place was nursery land and what exciting games we used to think out, for we were unusually intelligent and original children, I believe. Hide and seek, hunt the thimble, cobbler cobbler, kiss in the ring. Even Papa, who underneath his rather forbidding manner had all the enthusiasm of a boy, used to delight in playing this when he sometimes brought visitors up to the nursery, or even when alone. We had a very pretty nursery maid called Eva, with lovely golden curls and a face like a cherub. In fact we used to call her 'the Angel' because she looked exactly like a picture of angels saving a sheep from falling down a well, which hung in the nursery. Papa always insisted on her joining in too, for he was often quite democratic in his views I have noticed, so we were a splendid party. The mention of angels reminds me of a story of Mipsie which I specially love. One night she slipped out of bed and stole along to the day nursery to retrieve a favourite doll which Nannie had hidden as a penalty for some childish misdeed. But Mipsie knew just where it was—she was so clever in those ways—and also that Nannie would be downstairs having supper. However, she returned, to my surprise, without it—and looking rather thoughtful. Silently she climbed into bed. Then, after a pause: 'Blanche,' she said. 'Can angels sit on people's knees?' I considered the point, having always been interested in theology from a child. 'I don't really know, darling,' I remember saying, 'but I shouldn't *think* so.' 'That's just where you're wrong,' said Mipsie. 'They can' but not another word could I get out of her on the subject. What wondrous celestial vision had been vouchsafed to a child's innocent believing eyes that night, I wonder?

Most of our youth was spent in our historic and beau-

MIPSIE AT 'THE AGE OF INNOCENCE'

tiful home, but every summer we went to stay with some Scottish cousins, the McTott of Rum and Lady Agnes McTott on their beautiful island adjoining Eigg, my husband's native soil. It is strange to think I must have met him, for he often used to come over for picnics. Indeed, I remember a sturdy freckled boy finishing off a beautiful sand castle near us one day, and then my brother Humpo, who was adorably mischievous, taking a flying leap on to it! The older boy immediately put down his iron spade and picked up a bucket, so as to hit Humpo's head with something less heavy. I recollect, even at that early age, being struck by such gallantry.

Another memory of Rum comes back over the years, and one that still makes me shudder.

On that rocky and sometimes treacherous coast, the tide often turns unexpectedly and creeps in with the pace of a galloping snail. One day, I was lying on the shore absorbed in a book, when happening to glance up, I saw Mipsie, some twenty feet distant, perched on a big rock. Suddenly I remembered with horror that the tide was almost on the turn. In half an hour it might reach Mipsie's rock. In an hour it would undoubtedly have surrounded it.

What should I do? Should I go and tell Nannie, sitting beside the sleeping Humpo under the shade of the cliff near by? Or should I dash round the bay to the village and rouse one of the fishermen from his afternoon nap? But both courses would take time, and time was the vital factor. Within five minutes I had made up my mind. I would go to Mipsie's aid myself.

Swiftly I made my way over the sharp rocks and urged my little sister back, saying only that tea was ready, so as not to alarm her. When we reached Nannie I sank down, I remember, trembling a little with shock. But youth is resilient, and a good tea soon put me right.

As we ate it though, I watched the cruel waves coming nearer and ever nearer to the rock on which Mipsie had stood so lately. When we left the beach some forty minutes later I glanced back. The rock was entirely covered. I breathed a little prayer of thankfulness as I looked at my beloved sister, dancing gaily ahead, blissfully unconscious of her amazing escape from a terrible death.

III

DIFFICULT YEARS

'WHEN a man marries his troubles begin,' runs the old saying, but a woman's troubles begin far sooner, especially if she is beautiful, and poor Mipsie was soon to learn something of the unkindness and misunderstanding from a harsh world which is ever the lot of fair women.

The first unlucky incident was in 1886, when she was fifteen. A new curate—a Mr. Basil Simpson—had just come to Balder. Young, extremely handsome and a fine preacher, he was also exceptionally modest, and seldom looked up from the book of sermons which he read so delightfully. When he did, it was to encounter, in the front pew, the rapt and fervent gaze of one, at any rate, of his hearers. Mipsie, at an impressionable age, was just beginning to experience the emotions and aspirations of budding womanhood. What more natural than that she should be deeply stirred by this new influence? My mother welcomed the signs of a serious outlook in one who, though sweet, had been inclined to be frivolous hitherto, especially when the change was accompanied by a touching humility. Although our religious instruction was all that could be desired—having been undertaken by Mama herself—Mipsie declared that she would 'like to begin all over again,' and begged to be allowed to attend Mr. Simpson's Sunday classes. Accordingly, she and I went every week, for an hour—and then very often Mipsie would think of some point on which she needed further enlightenment, and would make me wait at the door of the Church Hall while she ran back to her instructor. She had, of course, even at that age, a fine sensitive mind which took a deeper view than did my humbler brain.

So passed spring and summer and eventually we came to Harvest Festival, in which of course we, as the great house, invariably played a predominant part.

My eldest sister Soppy[1] was always in charge of church decorations. None knew better than she just how to choose the softest evergreens for the lectern at Christmas, so that my father could read the lessons without being pricked (she kept the holly for the choir), or that the vicar had a dread of anything that harboured earwigs. No one could make a sheaf of corn 'stay put' as she could. She was older than us so had had practise with the then fashionable hair 'chignons' of course.

But on this occasion Mipsie insisted on going too, so off the two girls went and returned, after three hours, tired but satisfied. What was our consternation, however, on entering our pew next morning, when the first thing that greeted our horrified gaze was a huge vegetable marrow, reclining against the curate's stall, painted in clear letters: 'I LOVE YOU' followed by two hearts intertwined and the initials M.C. and B.S.? Who was the perpetrator of the odious joke we never knew—doubtless some jealous village girl—but it was considered by Papa to be too invidious to pass unnoticed. Mr. Simpson was consequently removed, and lest Mipsie should be further subjected to tricks in such bad taste, she and I were sent, after over a hundred prospectuses had been perused, I believe, to Miss Clamp's well-known school in Shropshire.

It was strange, after always having had our own governesses to order about as we pleased to be one of an

[1] Sophia, Lady Hogshead.

MYSELF AND MIPSIE IN OUR TEENS

obedient crowd; to wash in a plain white toilet set without the familiar coronet, to walk on grass instead of lawns. Strange—but not unpleasant. The girls were dears and I made lasting friends with several, even one who was a brewer's daughter, though I fear I kept this from Mama! But she afterwards married a baronet so all ended well. As for Mipsie, she soon became a little queen in the school, and whatever she did became the fashion. But once again, alas, her very charm and outstanding personality led to trouble.

The pupils' reading was very strictly guarded by Miss Clamp. Nothing in the nature of a novel was allowed to enter the school, let alone magazines, which were considered dangerous in the extreme. This struck Mipsie as narrow minded—she was ever the champion of liberties of all kinds—and she soon started to collect books by Ouida, Miss Braddon and others, also to write regularly to *The Girl's Own Mag.* under *nommes de plume* such as 'Bashful Husband', 'Enquiring Kitten' or 'Keyhole Kate', the letters being posted through the agency of a servant. The replies and the novels Mipsie kept in an old chest in a boxroom. There was a big demand naturally—in fact Mipsie was forced to charging sixpence for loans, which worried me a little till she told me she was saving the money for foreign missions. She was thus the founder of all lending libraries, only for a worthy cause—a typical stroke of genius.

All would have continued well, had not the oak chest been needed for some theatricals. The unusual weight aroused suspicion, the lock was forced open (for Mipsie kept the key) and the contents were discovered!

It was her sweet unselfishness that saved my sister. For she had had, a few days previously, that kind of presentiment that sometimes comes to brilliant people, that she might not be long in the school. Accordingly she had inscribed the name of every girl in the school—except ours—on the fly leaves of every book, so that each schoolfellow should have some memento of her. It was a generous and loving act which repaid the donor a thousandfold; for of course the books were not associated with her, and yet it was impossible to punish the whole school. Had Mipsie been a man she would surely have been an ambassador by now?

The whole episode would have passed with a stern reprimand, had it not been that right at the bottom of the chest were suddenly found—*two French novels*. Miss Clamp, I heard, fainted right off at the discovery. When she recovered she summoned the whole school. 'Girls,' she said sternly, 'this matter is no longer one of indiscretion and unladylike behaviour. It is one of crime. It must be sifted to the very bottom.'

IV

FINISHING TOUCHES

THE night after the discovery of the hidden books, including the two French novels, I slept badly, tossing and turning in my worry about what an investigation might bring to my poor innocent sister. Suddenly I woke to find her beside me, the candle lighting up her lovely hair, which was very luxuriant, hanging well below her neck and always shining with a perfectly natural grease.

'Get up and pack your trunks, Blanche,' she whispered. 'We are leaving to-morrow.'

'Leaving!' I gasped. 'But why?'

'I will not have any one wrongfully accused of hiding French novels,' said Mipsie staunchly. 'We must leave as a protest.'

So next morning we marched, she boldly, I in some trepidation, into the headmistress's sanctum.

'My sister and I are leaving,' announced Mipsie. 'We do not care to be associated with a scandal in any school.' Miss Clamp went as white as her shirtfront.

'But, Millicent,' she protested. 'No reflection was cast upon you or your sister. Yours were the only names not found in the books.'

'No matter,' said Mipsie. 'It is a deeply shocking occurrence, and I shall tell my Mama and Papa that we were unable to remain in such surroundings.' Miss Clamp turned as grey as her hair.

'Pray, pray, Lady Millicent, do not do that,' she begged.

'It will reflect badly on the school if Lord and Lady Coot hear such a thing.'

Mipsie, who had turned to the door, paused on the threshold. 'Will you promise us that there shall be no investigation, and that this odious business shall never be mentioned again, then?' she demanded sternly. There was a moment's pause. Then:

'I promise,' said Miss Clamp, flushing as red as the exercise book in her hand.

When we eventually left school, we were warmly embraced by the teachers and given quite a little ovation by the girls, some of them giving us lovely parting presents which they had made themselves—a beautifully-enamelled drainpipe parasol-stand for Mipsie, and a photo frame with real lace curtains for me. What a thrill to unpack these, and our prizes, and gloat over them. Suddenly, in Mipsie's pile of books, I saw, to my astonishment, the two confiscated French novels!

'Mipsie!' I gasped. 'However—wherever?' Mipsie smiled her most elfin smile.

'I knew just where to look for them,' she said. 'They were by Miss Clamp's bedside.'

There now followed a rather 'odd job' period of governesses for Mipsie alone, as I was eighteen and just about to come out. The trouble with these well-meaning but touchy people was my brother Humpo, who was, of course, a decided tease. During term he was at Eton (though he was nearly expelled for damping all the fireworks for the Fourth of June), but in the holidays the troubles began—specially with the French governesses. How Mdlle. Pinard screamed when she found her powder-puff full of wood lice!—it served her right for her Frenchified ways, Humpo said, with that subtle satiric wit that distinguished him even at that age. And how we screamed—but with laughter—when Mdlle. Boudin opened a box which she thought contained a new jacket, and found—a dead cat! She was ill for days!

Eventually, after ten or twelve governesses, Mipsie implored to be allowed to complete her French education in Paris. Mama opposed this, I remember, fearing the dangers of foreign food and Roman Catholicism; but Papa, rather surprisingly, advocated it strongly, even volunteering to take and fetch Mipsie each time, staying a week or two in Paris till she felt 'settled in'. Accordingly, in the summer of 1888, Mipsie went to St. Germain 'to be finished'.

The use of this expression reminds me of an amusing story of an old gardener of ours called Bobbin, a path weeder I think (all our weeds were lovingly extracted by hand by our devoted garden staff—no weedkiller for them!). Bobbin asked me after Mipsie one day. 'Why,' I told him, 'she has gone to Paris to be finished, Bobbin,' 'Dear, dear, is that so?' asked the old man sympathetically. 'Her ladyship being what she is that wouldn't take long in Paris, I reckon.'

I don't remember many details of Mipsie's school life in France, as I was by then in the whirl of my first season. But her letters home were radiantly happy, and of course she did brilliantly in class, as usual, soon being head of the school except for nine others. She also started to take a sudden interest in music, and put in long hours in the solitary music room. 'I am advancing so fast, Blanchie,' she wrote, 'that I have now graduated from Fräulein Lauch to Monsieur Poirot, the wonderful young professor here.' Next winter she wrote even more enthusiastically, 'I am learning all the *études* with the professor, and love my lessons. Only Paris is dreadfully cold. But he is so inspiring, and such a great musician. Sometimes he sings "Your tiny hand is frozen" to me and acts it all too beautifully for words.'

She left somewhat suddenly in consequence of a stupid misunderstanding. Mipsie always adored history, and she was thrilled with the excursions to Versailles, St. Cloud and other places of historical interest. So immersed was she in the past that she took the trouble to find out just what part of the Bois de Boulogne Madame de Pompadour frequented every day, in the same blue dress, in order to attract Louis XV's attention, and spent one whole afternoon near the same spot in order to steep herself in the historical atmosphere. Unluckily she was seen by the head of the *pension* who, completely misconstruing Mipsie's action, demanded her instant removal. It is so like the narrow scholastic mind to fail in appreciation of the born student of history.

V

COMING OUT

WHAT an auspicious event this was in the good old days, and how different from the present time, when a girl's figure scarcely changes with her début, and young people seem old before their 'teens. 'Do you mind awfully if I cut Lords this afternoon, Grandpapa?' my grandson said to Addle just before the war at the Eton and Harrow. 'There's a new film I want to see.' I was somewhat shocked, I must confess, but Addle said nothing. Indeed, he is inclined to be taciturn during a cricket match, and often his only remark during a whole day is 'Wait till the end of the over, dear.' (I suppose he thinks, in his old-world, courteous way, that the players would have to stop their game if I get up from my seat. He is always so considerate.) I am very fond of watching cricket myself, when with a cushion and a congenial companion one can spend the pleasantest afternoon, chatting of times past and present.

To return to girls' figures in the 'eighties, what miracles of elegance and womanliness they were. The tiny waist, the soft curves above and below, the smart bustle behind. I must admit, though, that the right effect was not achieved without trouble and sometimes tears. Gone were the days my mother knew, when she used to lie on the floor while an exceptionally strong footman (blindfolded of course) used to place one foot in the small of her back and lace her up. But a figure was still sufficiently important, in 1889, for Elsie Rye (Lord

Peckham's elder daughter), on the eve of her coming out ball, to get her young sister to hammer in a croquet hoop round her waist while she lay on the lawn. Unfortunately the sister was then called in to bed and poor Elsie lay the whole night pinned to the damp grass and had pneumonia next morning. Another friend, Lady Mary Linsey-Wolsey, who had the misfortune to be very flat-chested, bethought her of wearing an air cushion inside her dress; but in the crush of a reception she unwisely mounted a chair—some one's hatpin punctured the air cushion, and the whole crowd looked on in horror while her corsage collapsed with a long whine.

Another trial was hair. Fashion demanded a hair style which needed great luxuriance of woman's glory, and although of course we Coots all had beautiful hair, others were not so blessed, and were forced to wear false switches or coils pinned on. (I hope my male readers will not be shocked to hear of this deception.) My cousin Clara Twynge was very unlucky in the management of hers. They kept slipping off, once into the offertory plate, and once into a jug of fruit cup at a ball, which added somewhat to her natural shyness. Indeed, between that and the fact that she was distinctly plain (I do not know why, for she was a close cousin of ours), she was scarcely ever asked for a dance, and some unkind girls dubbed her 'Cloakroom Clara' because she used to spend almost every evening in that sad spot. Eventually Mipsie heard of this, and with her usual warm-hearted sympathy soon put things to rights. At the next ball, when Clara entered the ballroom, all eyes were drawn to a card attached to her bustle: 'Still waters run deep.' That evening she was besieged with partners and received three offers of marriage, all of which, in her shyness, she accepted, which was fortunate as two of the suitors threw her over next morning.

LE DUC DE TIRE-BOUCHON

Even in that age of beautiful women Mipsie's entrance into Society created something of a sensation. '*Qui est cette demoiselle là?*' asked the French Ambassador, a great connoisseur of beauty. When informed he said simply '*Tiens*' and continued to look at Mipsie. Even his Gallic eloquence was silenced by such loveliness, it seems. The same evening H.R.H. the Prince of Wales—afterwards King Edward VII—was evidently much struck with her. She happened, in the supper-room, to drop her fan almost at his feet. In a flash he had picked it up and handed it to her. A few minutes later she tripped on the staircase (she trips very easily I have often noticed) and his was the hand that came to her rescue. 'You are unfortunate this evening, Lady Millicent,' the Prince said gravely, while Mipsie blushed vividly at the compliment implied. A royal memory for faces is well known of course, but Beauty in Distress had evidently made an indelible impression on her future sovereign.

But, indeed, Mipsie was always the pet of Royalty. Her flashing wit and brilliant repartee often saved some difficult situation and turned a frown from a Royal brow. I remember one party at the Royal Yacht Squadron garden during Cowes week, when the somewhat austere King Crustatian of Iceland was the guest of honour. A sudden thunder shower had turned all the milk sour and H. M. was disposed to be annoyed, when: 'There shouldn't be any shortage of milk at *Cowes*,' said Mipsie audaciously. The Royal displeasure suddenly melted into a smile while every one blessed Mipsie for the quick wit that relieved the tension.

On another occasion she was able to do great service to her country by saving an Eastern potentate from an embarrassing episode. During a house party at the Duc de Tire-Bouchon's lovely château for the Chantilly Races, the vastly rich Great Curd of Bokhara had ordered a beautiful butterfly brooch to be carried out in rubies, amethysts and emeralds, the Duc's racing colours, as a gift for the Duchesse. This lovely jewel was to be placed, as a charming whimsy, in a naturalistic manner amongst the flowers at dinner. But the jeweller had made a mistake and used sapphires instead of amethysts. There was a nervous pause while every one looked at the butterfly and wondered what was wrong, for the Curd's face was like thunder. Then Mipsie, suddenly realizing the situation, took the brooch and swept him a deep curtsey.

'I am honoured, your Highness,' she said, 'both by the gift and by your gracious memory of our armorial colours.' It was a brave, splendid lie (for the Briskett colours are red and silver), told so as to save a foreign power from embarrassment. Relations were distinctly strained between our two countries at the time, so who knows what political strife, or worse, may have been averted by her noble action? But that is not the only time my dear sister, by her tact and brilliance, has helped her country, I am proud to say. At one time she was known as 'The Foreign Office Bag,' so many statesmen and State secrets did she hold in the palm of her lovely hand.

VI

ENGAGEMENT

ALTHOUGH my dear father and mother naturally wished to see their daughters married well, they were sufficiently idealistic in their attitude to matrimony to leave us entirely free in our choice, only stipulating that we should marry into the peerage (indeed we scarcely knew any one outside it so this was a needless precaution) and that our future husbands should have not less than £10,000 a year, so that we should be spared the misery of finding out for ourselves that 'Love flies out of the window when Economy comes in at the door' as the old saying goes. 'Ah, my dear,' I recollect an elderly lady saying to me when I was about twenty years of age. 'No one who hasn't experienced it knows the agony of soul that poverty and squalor bring.' She was speaking of the sale of their beautiful steam yacht which had to be effected before her husband could purchase one slightly larger.

My father was perhaps slightly more ambitious for his children than Mama was. I remember his referring to a certain German Prince who sought Mipsie's hand as 'jumped-up eighteenth century Royalty' and on another occasion he nipped in the bud what might have been a serious romance between myself and the very eligible Lord Gordon Dramm, heir to the marquisate of Deoch and Dorris. 'Gor,' in spite of his strict Scottish upbringing, had grown up decidedly unconventional, and was rumoured to be friendly with writers and even, some said, *artists*, though it doesn't do to believe all one hears.

Apart from this there was nothing serious against him, and he was the jolliest person imaginable, entering into every social function with great gusto and spirit. He had begun to single me out for special attention (giving me once, with lithe impetuosity, a sprig of white heather), and it must be admitted that I was equally taken with him. But one evening, at a dance at my old home, Coots Balder, I was waltzing with another partner and looking out (as girls will!) for my special admirer, when I saw a sight that froze the bones in my marrow. Gor was waltzing with another girl—and *he was reversing*! Immediately the dance finished I fled to my room and flung myself on my bed in floods of tears. Next morning Gor left, after a stinging rebuke from Papa, who afterwards told me never to mention the name of 'that bounder' again. It all shows what can happen to the best people by getting into the wrong company. Now, of course, I bless Gor for that solecism. I am sure my dear Addle has never done anything dishonourable or ungentlemanlike in his life. (Apart from anything else, he has never been sufficiently quick on his feet to manage the waltz at all.)

Perhaps it would be of interest to quote here two letters of my father's and mother's concerning Mipsie's future, which show the infinite and loving care with which parents in those days watched over their children's lives.

House of Lords, October 3rd, 1890.

MY DEAREST ARABELLA,

'I have made inquiries about young Harborough. He has 15 thou. it is true, but his estate is heavily encumbered, and his pedigree cattle and his mother cost him too much. They say Ld Skein is a warm man. He is too old for an heir probably, so Mipsie could marry again when he dies, or better still live with us and could enlarge the west wing as I have always planned. On the whole, however, I favour Briskett, even if his money is made in meat. He has the best moor in Scotland and a fine house in town next door to my club.

'Yr affectionate husband,

'C.'

Coots Balder, Oct. 6th.

'MY DEAR BOGGLE (my mother's pet name for Papa),

'I recd your letter yesterday and hasten to reply. Dearest, do you really think that the Duke of Briskett would make Mipsie happy? Money is not everything, and I cannot bear to think of our dear girl in those stone corridors at Briskett Castle. I know I should never feel anything but shivery there myself. Have you thought about young Ld Bodmin? Such a lovely place, as good as the Sth of France (you know what a shocking sailor I am) and I hear he is a nice young man, though illiterate they say, but of course Mipsie would manage all his affairs for him. I beg you not to decide in a hurry. Mipsie's happiness is all that matters to both of us, I know.

'Yr devoted,

'NIBBLES.'

(My father's pet name for Mama.)

'PS.—I am told the Bodmin fishing is superb.'

Eventually, as all the world knows, Papa's wishes for Mipsie's future prevailed over those of my mother, and my sister became engaged to 'Oxo' Briskett. She herself seemed oddly indifferent on the subject. I recollect her saying, with a strange bitterness for one so young, that she was beginning to find out that all men were made on much the same pattern. Yet I think she was happy in those engagement days. We used to have great fun opening the shoals of beautiful presents in the Orangery. Mine was the task of jotting down the shop labels on each present, so that they could be returned later if desired, for Mipsie was far too considerate to return them to the donors direct. Apropos, I cannot resist concluding with an amusing story of Mipsie's only slip in thanking for a gift.

It chanced that two Royal Dukes had both sent her a cake basket, Duke A's being of gold and Duke B's of silver. Mipsie *muddled up the Dukes* (an easy mistake to make) and wrote the following to Duke B.

'I shall think of your Royal Highness every time I use your beautiful gift, which will be daily, as I love gold filigree above everything, and although I have been given a silver basket shall never look at it, for it is far inferior in workmanship and material to your Royal Highness's.'

A second exquisite gold filigree cake basket arrived by special courier next morning!

VII

MARRIAGE

Of Mipsie's wedding day I can say little, for I myself was in such a whirl that I actually walked up the aisle after her in goloshes with my dainty peacock merino bridesmaid's dress! The service was solemn and beautiful in the extreme, every stone of the lovely old Balder Church, set off to perfection by the cream of Debrett, every flower that Heaven—and our famous hothouses—had created, reflecting the splendour of the occasion. Yet it was all quite simple. Two bishops and one archbishop only performed the ceremony. A humble bandsman from Oxo's regiment played 'Ave Maria' on the bass trombone; while the bridegroom, for all his wealth and many titles, stood alone, save for his best man, at the chancel steps, just like any ordinary wedding. Thus, in that simple country setting, my sister Mipsie gave her hand to a man who never really attempted to understand her, or to appreciate her amazing qualities.

Things really started going wrong, Mipsie tells me, as early as their honeymoon, which was spent at Kings Maunders, the beautiful and romantic home of Lord Dotage, which had been lent for that supposedly happy time. One afternoon, Oxo could not find Mipsie anywhere and after a long search discovered her in a spinney talking to a young man who rented some of the shooting, under the impression that it was her husband. The two men were of much the same height, both fair with small moustaches, and Mipsie had only been married two days.

It wasn't such a very serious mistake to make—but Oxo immediately took umbrage, as he always did at the adorable vagueness which was part of her charm.

The next quarrel was about the house. It must be explained that although the dukedom of Briskett was comparatively recent, the family of Loigne[1], as Earls of Chine[2], had lived in historic Briskett Castle in Northumberland since the Conquest. Queen Elizabeth had stayed awake all one night in the State bedroom[3], King Charles II[4] had shot an oak-apple off his brother's head in the park, Perkin Warbeck[5], as a scullion in the Briskett kitchens, had served up the meal which caused Henry VII[6] never to smile again. Several well-known ghosts also lived there.

But fine though the castle undoubtedly was, it was an austere and depressing place for a young bride of nineteen, and Mipsie can hardly be blamed for attempting to cheer it up somewhat. Her faultless taste naturally led, after her recent stay in Paris, to French décor, and so she had graceful Louis Quinze legs fitted on to the clumsy oak refectory tables, the fan vaulting of the Great Hall painted in the style of Boucher, and turned one of the dungeons into a *Salle des Glaces* as a compliment to Versailles, besides making a torture chamber into a very cosy little visitors' bathroom. She also gave orders for sprays of orchids to hang from the vizors of the suits of mail—for she just couldn't live without orchids, so great was

[1] Sometimes spelt Loyne or even Lohoyoillen.

[2] The Eighteenth Earl was awarded a dukedom for his brilliant work in remembering the names of all Queen Anne's children.

[3] The last person who actually slept there was Oxo's grandmother, who afterwards died of a fractured pelmet.

[4] Also dead.

[5] See Lambert Simnel.

[6] Who completed the famous chapel at Westminster, begun by Henry VIII during the Reformation.

her love of Nature—and bunches of carnations and roses to be placed daily in the jaws of the various skin rugs which lay all over the castle, for Oxo's father had been a keen big-game hunter. When Oxo seized an armful of these lovely blossoms and threw them into the fire, Mipsie immediately realized, with her delicate feminine intuition, that he was displeased, and essayed to mend matters by taking the best rug in the collection, a magnificent snow leopard, and having it made into a cloak in compliment to the father-in-law she had never seen. Could graceful tact go further? But this only seemed to make Oxo more angry still. He forbade her to alter the castle any more, saying that what was good enough for his ancestors was good enough for him. 'Of course, dear. Too good.' Mipsie said soothingly, but for some unaccountable reason that charming tribute to his forefathers was the last straw. Oxo flung himself out of the room, as he went breaking off the ormulu top which Mipsie had had fixed to a Saxon halberd and hurling it out of the window. It was their first real quarrel.

I have mentioned the Briskett ghosts. These included the headless third earl, who was said to walk the long gallery every night. For generations a beaker of brandy and a biscuit had been laid out for him each night by the butler. Brandy and biscuit were always gone by morning. But Oxo's mother, who was Scottish, thought the custom extravagant and silly and stopped it. The butler immediately gave notice. It is rather touching to think how much family tradition meant to servants in those good old days.

Then there was at one time a white stable cat which was said to have jet-black kittens every time one of the Loigne family died. But there was, I believe, some other explanation of that phenomenon not connected with the supernatural. Lastly, there was the famous Red Sultan, whom Mipsie actually saw.

The sobriquet was given to the seventh Earl for his oriental habits and character, which were known for miles around. He was eventually murdered by an irate farmer who discovered his daughter—a maidservant in the castle—dancing on the dining table before Lord Chine, dressed entirely in strings of coral. The ghost, apparelled in gorgeous Eastern robes and smoking a hookah, is said to haunt a room in the North Tower, which is consequently never used. But one day, both Mipsie and 'Weed' Wastrel (Sir Arthur Wastrel, an old admirer of hers, so nicknamed for his habitual cigar), announced their intention of keeping watch for one night in the haunted room. They tossed—and Mipsie won 'first go'. Next morning she declared that the Red Sultan had indeed appeared, but her description of him was so vague that a sceptic might have thought she had dreamed the whole thing, but for one curious circumstance. A thick, strongly-scented ash was found on the carpet afterwards, somewhat reminiscent of cigar ash, but doubtless emanating from the ghostly hookah. So I think there can be no doubt but that my sister really did receive a visitation that night.

VIII

SABLES AND A STARVED SOUL

THERE is many a lonely heart beating beneath a diamond parure. Golden lorgnettes may conceal tear-dimmed eyes. Underneath a chinchilla rug white hands may clench till their knuckles shine like knuckle-bones in the effort of self-control over some slight, some wounding hurt. . . . This was my poor sister's fate in those early days, when all the world seemed to smile on her and only her intimates knew that Life for her was a hollow mockery.

In those days, of course, an unhappy marriage was screened from the prying eyes of Society by a dignified façade, instead of being paraded before the whole world as it is to-day. For twenty years poor Blousie Banting, (Lady Louise Banting), wore heavy oriental bracelets to conceal the cruel bruises which her husband made by gripping her wrists because—although a brave man in other directions—he was terrified of going upstairs to bed. Lord and Lady Slough of Despond never spoke to each other after their honeymoon, yet the little notes which they wrote to each other on household matters were models of old-world courtesy and always written on the best note-paper. Nowadays what a change do we see! 'How I do dislike my husband,' a young married peeress, who had better be nameless, said to Addle at a dinner party shortly before the war. My husband, unable to believe his ears, thought she must be talking of dustbins and replied: 'Smelly things, I believe'—a remark which puzzled her exceedingly. But to return to Mipsie.

I only wish I could have helped her more during those difficult times, but I myself married before long and was naturally absorbed in my own happy home. Addle too, though the soul of chivalry as a rule, somehow lacked a finer perception of my sister's rare character. I remember recounting to him how I had found Mipsie in tears one day over one of Oxo's typical acts of brutal, freakish humour. She had, the previous week, suddenly realized that she could not meet all her bills out of her allowance, which, though adequate, had its limits, unfortunately. Punctilious to a fault, she had immediately passed them on to her husband, but, in order to soften the slight shock they might cause (for the total was a big one), she packed them in an empty cigar box of his favourite brand and sent it through the post. Oxo said nothing, much to Mipsie's relief, which changed to joy and gratitude the following day when she found on the hall table a package addressed to her in her husband's handwriting, containing—a morocco tiara case! Eagerly she unfastened the catch, only to find an empty case stuffed with the receipted bills. Her bitter disappointment may well be imagined. Yet Addle, when he had heard the piteous story, only remarked 'Good chap, Briskett', and changed the subject. How loyal men are to each other and how insensitive are the best of them to these little barbs that pierce the gentler sex.

Mipsie found consolation in intellectual and artistic interests, and especially in helping on young adventurers in both fields. 'Another of Mipsie's musical pursuits,' I once heard Oxo mutter, when my sister had sprung up and impulsively followed from the room a handsome and talented violinist who had just played exquisitely at a soirée. 'What do you want with these fiddlers?' he asked crossly when she returned. 'Fiddling is better than nothing,' replied Mipsie simply. But I happened to glance down at her lap. She was tearing a delicate seed pearl rope into a thousand shreds.

Thus life continued, inwardly so sad, outwardly so gay. Who will ever forget the Chine House receptions, where ambassadors fought with premiers for ices, and even Royalty lost hairpins, if nothing worse, in the crush? Mipsie's cotillions were always the gayest in London, her favours the most lavishly bestowed. A minor war was started because a certain potentate put his empty plate down on a neighbouring Begum's bare shoulder, mistaking it for a mahogany slab. A long political quarrel was healed when the two statesmen concerned found themselves wedged for a whole evening between a marble Diana and her stag. Mipsie herself was a dominating influence in politics and the confidante of many great men. 'Will there be war, Lord Salisbury?' she boldly asked the premier at the time of the Boer troubles. 'I sincerely hope not, Duchess,' he replied, 'but it is an event that must always be considered a possibility.' Such frankness at such a time shows his trust and high opinion of my sister.

Speaking of foresight over wars reminds me of a delightful story of my dear husband, which I cannot resist telling in conclusion. During the Munich crisis Addle, who is one of the most far-seeing men I know, suddenly realized that the European situation was far from calm, and with that thought he began to worry whether his beloved country was fully prepared for the event of war. He conceived the wise and splendid plan that there should be some form of officers' training corps at public schools, so that the boys who were the future upholders of our race should learn, as he put it simply, 'to hold a rifle like a gentleman.' He spent many months in working out the whole scheme, which he proposed to put to the Lords when completed, and actually got as far as going over to Eton, his old school, to consult the headmaster on the subject. It entailed missing his afternoon nap, but Addle is not the man to shrink from duty. At Eton however, he discovered to his amazement that there is actually a system installed on very similar lines at every public school, only it had slipped his memory. Furthermore, a school contemporary of his whom he happened to meet, taking his great grandson to Rowlands, reminded Addle that he himself had been in the shooting eight one year, when Eton had won the Ashburton Shield. But the lofty idea and the work the scheme entailed remain the same, even though others had thought of it before. It is just another case of 'great minds thinking alike'.

IX

THE FINAL RIFT

WHAT can be more despicable than *noblesse* which does not *oblige*, a duke with the soul of a commoner, a coronet with balls of clay? These epithets—and worse if there be any—might well be showered on my brother-in-law, Oxo Briskett, for refusing the common courtesy of giving grounds for divorce (on the futile plea that the only grounds he knew were those of his own park) and subjecting my poor sister to that humiliation instead. I will spare my dear readers the bitter details, for I have already told the whole sad story in my first book *Lady Addle Remembers*. Suffice it to say that Mipsie found herself in 1903 alone, stripped of everything, including her good name and her pearls, robbed of her children except for six months of the year, struggling to keep body and soul together on the pittance of £3,000 a year which Oxo allowed her. 'I feel outlawed,' she wrote to me from her suite at the Crillon during the first months. My immediate reply was to beg her to leave Paris and make her home with us at Bengers. She accepted gratefully. 'All that I want is to be quiet and to get to know which are my own children,' I remember her saying when she arrived.

Her delightful pair—Ferdy and Millie—were slightly older than my two toddlers, James and Hector, but the four were as devoted as cousins can be, and except for Ferdy trying to drown James—but only in fun—and Millie (an adorable little imp, the image of Mipsie) tying up Heccy with skipping ropes one day and hitting him in the face with stinging nettles until he gave her his pearl horse-shoe pin, they were as happy as the day was long. I was upset with Millie for that episode I must confess, and I recollect insisting to her mother that the child must either give Heccy back his pin or be punished. Mipsie was adamant. 'There is no question about which course is right,' she said firmly. 'Millie must be punished.'

Nowadays, of course, the upbringing of children has greatly changed, and I dare say we should be considered old fashioned in our methods. My dear Margaret, who now has the happiest reasons for studying child psychology writes to me that she is very interested in a new theory called, apparently, 'Inverted Sin'. I don't really understand it very well but I fancy the idea is that all childish naughtiness is in reality moral qualities trying to find self-fulfilment. Thus, breaking things is the unconscious desire to break down social barriers, telling lies is the imagination seeking an outlet for expression, bullying and unkindness is the ego searching for self-reliance, and greed is just generosity 'beginning at home'. So the child is encouraged to bully and lie, is given something new to break each day and supplied with plentiful opportunities for over-eating. In that way the real self is not repressed and grows out of the cocoon of a disagreeable child into a fine man or woman. Though there are, I understand, fairly frequent cases where the early training takes a hold and is not discarded in later years.

It all seems a trifle too modern to me, but anyway I am sure I shall love my grandchild, however my dear Margaret decides as to his or her future upbringing.

But to return to Mipsie and her sojourn at Bengers. Happy as this was it was not long before she began, very naturally, to long for 'some tiny corner of my own to call home,' as she touchingly put it, and she took, as a little *pied-à-terre*, a house in Park Lane, furnishing it entirely from Bengers, 'so'—she expressed it—'as to have something tangible to remember her dear sanctuary by.' I thought this such a beautiful idea, and was also glad in her straightened circumstances to be able to help her in a small way financially, but I was never absolutely certain that Addle saw it in quite the same light. 'How long is Mipsie staying with us?' he asked once during the transition stage between town and country. When I said: 'For as long as she wants to, I hope. Why?' my husband replied: 'I was wondering if we'd have anything left to sit on soon.' This referred, I guessed, to the fact that my boudoir, where we were sitting at the time, was indeed rather chair-less, because Mipsie had lost her heart to the Heppelwhite set which had been there, and the new set I had ordered to replace them had not yet been delivered. I had tried to make things look better by having some packing-cases moved up and draping them with *petit point*, but I fear Addle, who was sitting on one, may have noticed the difference. So in some trepidation I asked 'You do like Mipsie, don't you, dear?' and went on to tell him that only that morning I had had a letter from Oxo in which even he referred to Mipsie's 'taking ways.' My husband smiled and nodded. 'Taking ways is just the right description,' he said, and I felt happy again, realizing that he, too, was a victim to my sister's ineffable charm.

But Mipsie was destined never to dwell in that little Mayfair nest. The reason for her change of plans was a sermon we heard in Great Bengers church from a visiting missionary, just back from India. He discoursed on the great contrast that existed between the poor outcastes among India's teeming millions and the immensely rich Princes, in their palaces like abodes from the Arabian

Nights. Mipsie listened, her eyes gleaming with sympathy for the untouchables, and after the service she sought me in my bedroom.

'Blanchie,' she said, 'I have been wrong in thinking in such a small circumscribed way, when there is so much to see, so many of the world's treasures for all to share. I am going to India, where the thought of such wrongful distribution of wealth haunts me. Perhaps—who knows—I can help to even out those cruel inequalities.'

Within a week she had sold the Park Lane house with all its contents so as to pay for the journey which, as my dear readers will soon see, extended far beyond India. She was thus one of the first cultured women (by which of course I mean English women) to go, alone and unprotected, into the far corners of the globe. Did I say unprotected? No, for such was the appeal of her beauty, her courage, her very helplessness, that wherever she went protectors seemed to spring up, as if by magic, at her side.

X

PASTURES NEW

MIPSIE'S Indian tour started off in the most dramatic manner, as things have a way of doing in her vivid and colourful life, I have noticed. She had scarcely reached India's shores when a message arrived from the all powerful Rajah of Badsore, begging her to accept the use of his motor throughout her visit. It was in the early days of motoring when cars were very liable to break down, so the vehicle was accompanied by a huge royal elephant, richly caparisoned and bearing a jewelled howdah, who lumbered behind the car at the then daring pace of fifteen miles an hour. It was a wise precaution. For in going up a steep incline the car suddenly jibbed—then to the horror of the accompanying train of servants, commenced to run back right into the elephant's hairy chest! Mipsie was quite unperturbed. 'An elephant's chest is a welcome change after my husband,' she records in the journal which she kept throughout the tour. A moment later she felt herself being reverently lifted up by the noble beast and deposited in the howdah, none the worse except for the loss of her motor veil, which he ate. 'Evidently,' she adds, 'an elephant never forgets the British aristocracy.'

The Rajah's A.D.C. apologized humbly for the veil's disappearance and promised that his royal master would present her with another. So touched was Mipsie by this that she immediately descended and offered the elephant her gloves and dustcoat. All three articles were subsequently replaced—and the best that money could buy of course—by His Highness.

Soon she arrived at the fabulous saffron palace, which is now well known to tourists. Tier upon tier of bright yellow marble turrets towered high above the town of Badsore, while all the rugs, furniture and curtains were of the same tint, which is the royal colour and therefore cultivated by tradition to such an extent that the women in the Zenana all wear yellow *saris* and tint their eyelids, etc., with saffron. There was a story that an English girl, staying in the neighbourhood, was once stricken with jaundice. The Rajah happened to see her—had her kidnapped and—so great was his admiration—even contemplated marrying her. Time passed, however, and the girl recovered. The Rajah, in disgust, had her thrown off a 500-foot parapet to some starving jackals, after which unhappy incident I believe she died.

Unfortunately, at the time of Mipsie's visit, the Rajah was in failing health from saffron poisoning, so my sister was only able to see him once. He had been a man of vast appetite, but was on a diet of not more than eight chickens and one pea-hen a day. As he ate the yellow flesh—for they were of course cooked in saffron—Mipsie was fascinated to see him throw the bones over his shoulder out of a window. On asking H. H. the reason for this he told her that his people waited below for anything he had touched, which was considered sacred. Fearing that she might suffer the same fate, Mipsie quickly said: 'I should be honoured if your Highness would also present me with a keepsake.' For answer the Rajah held out his hand. 'Take this,' he said. 'Men have died to gain it'—and he handed her a pea-hen's eye. Only Mipsie's ready wit saved her from having to accept the unpleasant object. 'I regret, your Highness,' she said, 'that my religion forbids me certain parts of pea-hens.'

The Rajah respected her code and presented her with a magnificent yellow emerald instead.

Mipsie went on to stay—in great contrast to the Rajah of Badsore—with the gentle and cultured Marharaj Rana of Singhit Bunji, who, born of a warrior race in which every prince of the blood had, on attaining his fifteenth birthday, to prove his merit by killing 50 tigers, 50 leopards and either 100 sambur or 200 natives, revolted against this butchery, became a Christian, and a vegetarian and joined the R.S.P.C.A. Subsequently he made a law in his province that no one should take life. This had its disadvantages as, of course, even vermin was preserved, and the fleas wore gold collars and were encouraged to enjoy a good meal from high and low alike. The Marharaj Rana achieved wonders in the taming of beasts of prey and he invited Mipsie to go and see his favourite tiger who he was slowly converting to vegetarianism by placing near its lair exquisite silver dishes containing peaches, asparagus and cream cakes. The only thing that caused the animal to revert to type was, apparently, the sight of another tiger or other creature of prey.

Unfortunately the experiment proved a failure that time, as for some unaccountable reason the moment the tiger set eyes on Mipsie he began to snarl and roar, and so had to be driven away by the servants, leaving untouched a beautiful *ommelette aux fines herbes* and a *pêche Melba*.

Space forbids that I should describe the whole of Mipsie's Indian tour. There was the wonderful aviary palace of Hotgong, filled with birds of every species and hue, including the sacred parrots which were trained to screech every time the Newab of Hotgong approached. Mipsie said they made a fearful clamour, especially during the night. Then there was the Rajah of Ahgotodabad, with whom she stayed longest, whose fairy tale jewels extended even to the furniture. Mipsie had a vast bath mat, she says—too big to go into her trunk, (she tried)—encrusted round the border with precious stones of the first grade. On another occasion there was an amusing episode when her host had a visitor of equal rank staying with him, and as a matter of etiquette it was impossible to decide with whom an English duchess should go in to dinner. Mipsie solved it by sitting on the shoulders of one with her hands clasping the osprey on the other's turban (the osprey came off in her hands!). A very neat solution I think.

Eventually her tour came to an end. 'I am the richer by some wonderful experiences,' she wrote in her journal, 'but still I feel that the world is an oyster which has not really yielded me up its pearl,' and with that ideal in mind she decided to return to England via Arabia and Egypt, of which I shall write in the next chapter.

XI

FROM RED SEA TO BLACK TREACHERY

AT Aden Mipsie left the comparative comfort of her luxury liner and boldly embarked, entirely alone save for her secretary and courier, Major Hardup, her personal maid, and the captain and little crew of twenty, on the beautiful steam yacht which had been lent to her by a friend for the remainder of her trip.

Their first objective was Uassa Land, that picturesque little colony just above Eritrea which is ruled over by a line of Merchant Princes whose traditional generosity is only equalled by their devotion to England. It was these splendid qualities which appealed to my sister and which prompted her to ask Major Hardup, whom she met on the boat, and who had had considerable experience in native parts, to arrange the tour for her. He gladly accepted, enchained by her beauty at once, and also most grateful for the generous remuneration which she offered him, for he was on half pay with no private money, poor man. It is terrible to think there are such cases of hardship amongst British officers.

Mipsie's vivid journal describes their journey from Port Maggot on the Red Sea, up the famous Red Mite gorges to Nojoko, the capital.

'The sun rises here at four o'clock, spreading deep crimson and purple lights over the rocks, an unforgettable sight, the description of which made a deep impression on me as Major Hardup gave it at breakfast on my *crumpet* (hotel verandah) five hours later. I hastily swallowed coffee and *jim-jams* (native rolls) and caught the only train in the day, which leaves at ten a.m. As it is too hot to travel after ten-thirty we left the train at Badeg and waited for our *skivvi-bog* (procession of servants on donkeys) to catch up with us. All round us were wonderful flowering eggs, while brilliant yellow flying adders zoomed overhead. 'They are attracted by your face powder,' Major Hardup explained, 'but are quite harmless.'

'The natives will trade anything for toothpicks. We brought several thousand with us and purchased a good supply of *nitties*—a kind of banana-shaped pineapple, and plentiful *oompahs*—a delicious pineapple, looking and tasting exactly like a banana. Also emu's eggs and several bottles of *tjck*—the native fiery wine which the better caste tribes drink before killing their grandmothers, a regular custom on Friday nights at sundown. At Skrewi we were fortunate enough to see a native wedding, which was most interesting. The bride is entirely swathed in pampas gauze, while the bridegroom is clothed only in gourds, which are hung round him in such profusion that he can hardly move. While the villagers beat the *chummi* (a rude kind of gong) the local maidens slowly unwind the veiling and the bridegroom's friends, in a kind of leaping dance, remove his gourds one by one. It was thrilling to watch, and I found myself longing to take part, but Major Hardup said it would be a riot so firmly removed me, alas, before the ceremony was completed. I was told that the bride is usually so scratched by the pampas gauze and the bridegroom so bruised by the gourds that they are frequently unable to meet again for weeks. Divorce is very prevalent in Uassa land.'

At Nojoko Mipsie was met by Ras Bollinogud's servants and conducted with great ceremony to his palace. Here a

MIPSIE IN UASSA-LAND NATIVE COSTUME

bitter disappointment awaited her. Ever since she had arrived in Uassa she had been under the protection of the Prince, who had frequently intimated, in letters and through his agents, that a gift worthy of an English duchess awaited her at the capital. On the palace steps she was handed a paper listing 'the gift': '200 fat black sheep, 100 *yonghi* (the local blue oxen, born mad, considered a great delicacy eaten raw), 50 alligators' hides, 1 cwt. of incense and 10 jars of snake oil.' It was, from Ras Bollinogud's viewpoint, doubtless the most generous present, but to my sister it was naturally a blow, having expected something more portable and utilitarian, like precious stones or gold. However, with her unfailing good manners she thanked the Prince for his favour—then, with one of her impetuous gestures of reckless generosity, she turned to Major Hardup. 'These are for you,' she said in French. 'Your salary for the trip.' So overcome was her secretary by the gift—which was, of course, worth many times his due—that he had to sit down and ask for brandy. Indeed, he did not completely recover his equilibrium till they had left Nojoko and were on their return journey to Port Maggot. Then suddenly, while sipping their coffee outside a little *bumbar* (very homely estaminet) he surprised Mipsie by springing to his feet and exclaiming, with fear in his eyes as he spoke the words:

'We must get to the coast as soon as possible. Ras Bollinogud will be furious at our leaving his gifts behind. which is considered a grave insult to a host. We are in great danger.'

The warning of Ras Bollinogud's treachery came too late. When Mipsie turned her horrified gaze to the little village square behind her it was to see a crowd of natives approaching, their *pokos* (four-edged spears) gleaming in the sunlight, murder in their faces.

It was a terrible moment. Major Hardup, who to do him justice was ready to pay for his unforgivable lapse with his life, immediately sprang to Mipsie's side. But where blood is blue hearts are stout. She pushed him impatiently aside and standing to her full height, faced the angry people, holding in her hand an empty envelope.

'I have here,' she said in clarion tones, 'a letter to our Foreign Secretary, Sir Edward Grey. Beside me'—and she pointed with a firm hand)—'is a pillar box. Unless you go quietly to your homes I shall post this letter, and in less than two months the entire British Army will come to my aid, and you and your wives and children will be annihilated.'

The threat worked. The fire died out of their eyes and there was a great hush over the square. Then suddenly, a handsome young Uassan sprang up beside Mipsie.

'Three cheers for the Duchess and the British Foreign Office,' he shouted—and the little town rang with loyal cries.

Thus was the situation saved by a woman's courage and the world-wide respect commanded by the British aristocracy and the British Constitution.

XII

SLAVES OF DESTINY

WITH all her amazing beauty and charm, Mipsie is also far better educated than nineteen peeresses out of twenty. Thus it was that she had heard of the 'Thousand and One Nights,' and was determined to experience their delights for herself. Major Hardup, who of course knew the Arabians from end to end, eagerly agreed to conduct her once more.

Accordingly they landed at el Bismuth and proceeded by camel to the busy little town of Hamfist, famous for its dyes (which are made from crushed spiders, these insects being of every hue and as big as tennis balls). Mipsie and Major Hardup explored the market the first day and my sister was entranced by the brilliantly coloured costumes and draperies she saw and bought for herself a beautiful royal blue and jade green dress, heavily embroidered in gold beads, together with a pearl pink yashmak. These she donned next day, and delighted her secretary by giving him an imitation of an oriental dance on her wash-hand-stand! Then, much to his alarm, she announced her firm intention of sallying forth into the streets thus attired. He tried to dissuade her, but in vain, and all he could do was to follow her at a distance. Perhaps he had some premonition of the dreadful fate that awaited her?

For a time all went well. Mipsie threaded her way into the busy market-place un-noticed. Then suddenly she found herself in a ring of women, all dressed, as she was, in peasant finery, while there appeared to be some kind of auction in process, with a good deal of shouting and arguing in many strange tongues. Meanwhile, poor Major Hardup had quite lost sight of her amidst the thronging crowd. Time passed and he became more and more worried, so much so indeed that he had to return to their hotel and ask for brandy. His search continued far into the evening, until he had explored every corner of Hamfist and every restorative the town possessed. Eventually, from various sources, he pieced together the terrible history. A particularly powerful sheikh, Abdul Akrid bin Sniftah, had that day descended from his mountain castle and purchased a large consignment of female slaves, who had already been conveyed into captivity by bullock carts (though we learnt later that Mipsie had ridden on Abdul's own camel, the sheikh walking beside her). Major Hardup groaned aloud as he staggered into the hotel bar when the fearful truth broke upon him.

Mipsie had been sold into slavery.

What were our feelings when we received his cable I leave my dear readers to imagine. Even Addle, who seldom shows emotion, had no heart to shoot that day and spent the morning scratching his favourite pig's back and thinking of Mipsie in the sheikh's power. The awful part was that we could do nothing. Major Hardup had indicated that he was trying to redeem Mipsie by purchasing goats, which was the exchange most appreciated by a sheikh. But beyond cabling 'Buy to the limit,' we could only wait for news. When it came it seemed the end of hope. Major Hardup had offered 1,000 goats—an enormous price—but Abdul bin Sniftah flatly refused to part with my sister.

It is in such black moments that inspiration sometimes comes to pierce the gloom. Suddenly I saw clearly the only possible solution; my family's famous breed of Balder goats must be sacrificed. My father was unfortunately on one of his business trips in Paris, so Addle went post-haste to Coots Balder, empowered by him to give the word—which my brother Crainy[1], who was very seldom heard to speak at all, would find it almost impossible to utter—that would send out to Arabia as many of our beloved goats as might be necessary to buy my sister's freedom—ten, twenty, one hundred if need be. To our unutterable relief a cable came from the sheikh himself, after he had received a minute description of the goats, saying that he would release Mipsie in exhange for two. 'One woman is much the same as another but a new breed of goats is an occasion,' he is reported to have said—hardly a gallant remark, but we were all too overjoyed to cavil.

It was sad that Major Hardup was laid low with alcoholic malaria and could not go himself to conduct my sister back—doubly sad as it transpired, in that he sent as a deputy a friend of his Sandhurst days, Sir Constant Standing, who was in Arabia for the scorpion shooting. He immediately fell a victim to Mipsie's beauty, clearly visible even through her now torn garments, and she in her turn was attracted to him, for it was many weeks since she had seen a white man. Besides, Constant was undoubtedly good looking as well as being a fine soldier and a baronet of an old family. Noting that he seemed occasionally pre-occupied and worried, Mipsie, with her quick sympathy, soon drew him out and learnt that he was indeed concerned at the moment by the hourly expected death of his uncle, the enormously rich Lord Parsimony, who had declared him his heir. Pity, they say, is akin to love. Perhaps it was

[1] Viscount Crainiham.

this womanly emotion, perhaps it was relief at her freedom, or perhaps it was just Destiny, that had once made a slave of my sister and was now to cast her into the far more bitter slavery of a second unhappy marriage. However it may be, it was as Lady Millicent Standing that Mipsie embarked, after a primitive six weeks' honeymoon at Shepherd's Hotel, Cairo, to return to England and Home--she brought the Beauty with her.

XIII

A NEW INTEREST

As so often happens in life, the very strength and fervour of Mipsie's sympathy with her new husband over the grave illness of his millionaire uncle, Lord Parsimony, wore her out and made the old man's sudden recovery seem somehow like an anti-climax in which she was incapable of showing or even feeling any joy. In addition, it is well known that Lord Parsimony was a puritan of the deepest dye, who rigidly disapproved of divorce and consequently of his nephew's beautiful wife. In fact, Mipsie strongly suspected him of rallying simply in order to upset her, which would have been base and unkind behaviour indeed. However this may be, she felt sadly depressed and disillusioned on her return to England—a depression which was increased by many bitter letters from Major Hardup, still laid up in Hamfist, in which he accused her of discarding him like an old love. To counteract the effect of these sad episodes she decided on a few months in the South of France, as a mental pick-me-up for her and perhaps a financial pick-me-up for her husband, whose fortunes were very low after his uncle's unexpected recovery. 'Besides,' Mipsie said when she told me of the plan, 'Constant is such a keen sportsman. The pigeon-shooting will make up for his disappointment at missing his partridges this year.' I recount this little anecdote so that my dear readers may see that Mipsie at any rate intended to 'love, honour and cherish' in her second marriage.

It cannot be denied that gambling is in every Coot's blood. There are, indeed, many instances of this passion leading my family to strange and even desperate passes. The fourth Earl, in 1730, once played faro for five days and nights on end. When eventually he won a fortune from his opponent and essayed to rise—he could not move. His beard had grown round one of his own legs! On another occasion the Viscount Crainiham of the time, having wagered everything to another young blood (except Coots Balder, which was entailed), had nothing left to offer except his aunt, Lady Emily Coot, who was refused as being too old and ugly. When it was pointed out that she was possessed of a fortune amounting to five figures, the gambler wittily said: 'It's her own figure I object to.' However, he accepted the wager, which he won. He was then in a quandary as to how to take possession of a bed-ridden old lady of eighty-seven. Eventually he had her kidnapped (including her bed), and set about investigating her will. He found that Lady Emily, herself an inveterate gambler, had lost the whole of her fortune a few days previously to another octogenarian in a contest of who could turn round in bed the greatest number of times in an hour.

But to return to Mipsie. She and Constant settled down very happily at Monte Carlo, and for a time I hoped that their mutual interest of the tables—not that he was so keen on gambling—would draw them together into the serenity of a happy English family life. I confess that I did not greatly enjoy our only visit to them. Addle missed his pigs sorely, and caused rather an upset at the Casino by asking for the windows to be opened, and I kept on worrying about how the village would get on without me. But it is always an interesting experience to glance into a world outside one's own, and I was able to give a nice little talk on Monte Carlo to my Mothers'

Union when I returned—only fearing that the mention of gambling might have a harmful effect on their quiet lives, I pretended that nothing but halma was played—an innocent little deception which I hope my recording angel will forgive.

For a long time Mipsie's luck at the tables was amazing, and the talk of Monaco. Indeed, visitors seated round the roulette board used to hail my sister's entrance into the *salon* with delight and implore her to come and sit on them so as to bring them fortune. In one year she amassed over 200,000 francs, bought herself a string of pearls and allowed Constant to give her an ermine wrap. Then suddenly, fickle fortune changed and they had to see most of their gains disappear. Constant's ineptness, his inherent weakness of character now showed itself. Mipsie had done her share—it was obviously his turn to come to their rescue and make money, as she justly pointed out. Instead, he only continued to lose. 'You have no backbone, no system in life,' Mipsie told him with some bitterness. As a result, he spent much time on working out several systems which eventually led them both to disaster, as the following chapter will show.

I must end on a happier note—an amusing story of how Mipsie once acted as a pawnbroker! One day, on the terrace near the Casino, she chanced to see a young girl in tears, while a very handsome young man was endeavouring to comfort her. Mipsie, with her ready sympathy, immediately asked the cause. It was the same old story—they had lost every penny on their honeymoon and could not even pay their hotel bill. 'If only I could get back to Austria,' the girl wept, 'my father never denies me anything. But we haven't even the fare.' Mipsie patted her arm. 'Don't worry, my child,' she said soothingly. 'I will pay your fare for you.' The girl gasped: 'Madame! Will you really trust me?' Mipsie smiled her most roguish smile. 'No, my dear,' she said, 'but my husband will escort you to Austria and back and you shall leave your husband with me as security till you return.' Surely the most curious transaction that can ever have taken place in that romantic little Principality, but one that indeed testifies to my sister's warm and all-embracing heart.

XIV

FORTUNE'S WHEEL

CONSTANT was unfortunately no mathematician, and he would have been far wiser to admit frankly to this failing instead of attempting to work out systems for roulette and baccarat which were quite beyond his mental powers, and cost Mipsie thousands of francs in testing. It also meant a time of great loneliness for my poor sister, who would sally forth by herself each day after locking her husband into his room as a gentle encouragement to work.

During these months of enforced widowhood many strange and dramatic things happened to her, as is ever the way in her vivid life. One evening she was walking through the casino gardens when a certain Russian nobleman, a few yards ahead, drew his revolver and placed it to his temple! She was just in time to strike his hand away, so that the bullet sped harmlessly into a passing peasant. In gratitude, he gave her his magnificent sable-lined cape before taking prussic acid. On another occasion she became involved—innocently of course—in a daring plot to rob the casino. A rich Cuban had recently arrived in his luxury yacht and had aroused the interest of the whole of Monaco by his dark handsome features and flashing eyes, as well as by his strange, somewhat unusual habits, such as picking his teeth with a jewelled dagger. Mipsie, always fascinated by the bizarre, was equally keen to meet the stranger, but no one seemed able to effect an introduction. But my sister is nothing if not unconventional and impulsive—she once achieved acquaintanceship with a famous 'cellist by throwing herself at his feet and embracing his instrument—and she determined not to be beaten in this instance. Accordingly, she smuggled herself on board his yacht disguised as a great sheaf of madonna lilies, and thus attired posed on the dining table at a party which transpired to be entirely composed of men. To her astonishment, as the dinner proceeded, she heard discussed every detail of a daring plot to rob the *salle privée*. The only thing missing, apparently, was some one of irreproachable social standing, to give the gang the entrée to that millionaires' haven. Such was Mipsie's excitement at these words that several madonnas trembled and fell off her. The company, seeing what was beneath the snow-white petals, rose as one man, as the Cuban handed her down from the table and filled her to the brim with champagne.

'Gentlemen,' said Mipsie to gain time, 'I am at your disposal.'

Somehow or other the casino administration got wind of the plot, however, before Mipsie could warn them. The Cuban and his accomplices left Monaco as suddenly as they arrived and were never seen again. The curious thing is that when the former, in a rage, demanded who had betrayed them, the Chef de Sûreté replied enigmatically: 'Nobody, M'sieur. Our suspicions were aroused by the company you keep'—a remark that remains a mystery to this day. But when Mipsie sought an interview with the casino authorities and told them that she had intended to inform on the gang that very day, they only smiled and bowed her out. No large reward, as is customary when a fraud is exposed. Such is official gratitude.

After that, things went from bad to worse with Constant and my poor sister, who were often hard put to it to know where their next *mille* was coming from. Then suddenly, fortune's wheel turned once more. Constant, who was decidedly clever with his hands, had made himself a roulette wheel on which to test his systems. It was so much admired that there was quite a demand from their many friends for roulette wheels for private parties. Of course, not being an expert, it was impossible to make them absolutely true, but as Mipsie told him, that only added to their charm, like crazy beams in an old house (she has often told me how she loves anything crooked) and she also encouraged him to paint each one slightly differently, so as to give them distinction. Orders poured in, and things began to look up a little for Mipsie as with the money Constant made she played carefully and astutely at private parties only—for the casino had somewhat lost its charm since a system they had tried called the *coup de poivre*—which involved making the croupier sneeze at a certain point, I believe—had seemed in some way to annoy the management, who being foreigners had, of course, no sense of humour.

Then, without warning, the blow fell.

Mipsie had just broken the bank on one of Constant's wheels at a private party given by a Grand Duke, when to the astonishment of all, an American woman, who had lost heavily, accused my sister of playing on inside knowledge of the wheel.

Mipsie, like any loyal wife, appealed to her husband. 'Constant,' she demanded, 'are you going to sit there and hear me insulted?'

The incredible, the unforgivable thing then happened. *Constant said* '*Yes.*'

She left him next day and came, like a wounded bird, to Bengers. Even so she might have returned to him, for he wrote her a letter of abject apology, saying that he was so used to agreeing with her over everything that the words had automatically slipped out. But while she was considering what was best to do his uncle, Lord Parsimony, died and cut his nephew out of his will entirely. Mipsie felt that he must have had good cause, to take such a drastic step, since before his marriage to Mipsie Lord Parsimony had always declared his nephew to be his heir. 'If only I had known that he was really worthless I would never have married him,' poor Mipsie said bitterly, when I gave her the cheque for her divorce expenses, which her husband was unable to pay.

Constant has continued to go downhill, I fear. He lived on in the South of France, where a friend of Addle's saw him just before the war, clad only in old flannel trousers with nothing above them. 'What's happened to your shirt, Constant?' called out our friend. Constant's reply, in execrable taste, shows the depth of his descent. 'I put it on the wrong wife,' he is said to have answered.

XV

THE STRUGGLE FOR EXISTENCE

In 1908 Mipsie's chief problem was that of finance. Indeed this might be said to apply to almost every year of her brave, romantic life. Her pin-money of £3,000 a year from Briskett nowhere near sufficed to meet her commitments, and she had nothing else to fall back on, except her jewels, of which she gallantly refused to sell so much as one hatpin. I remember Addle coming upon her one day at Bengers (where she always lives in between husbands) laying out her collection on a stool for my benefit. 'Those your frozen assets, Mipsie?' he asked. My sister laughingly shook her head. 'My assets are never frozen,' she replied.

In those days, of course, no woman of the *beau monde* ever dreamed of earning her living, and indeed I strongly deprecate the custom which heavy taxation has forced upon us to-day. I shall never forget how shocked I was when an old friend of mine, Craggie Kruschen (Baroness Kruschen, a cousin of the Hapsburgs) came to see me a few years ago, saying she was on her way to work. 'What work?' I inquired. 'Oh, charring,' was the gay reply. 'I go every day and scrub for Pamela Pershore and she does the same for me. Our servants wouldn't respect us if we did our own houses.' As a matter of fact, Craggie had the best of the bargain, because the Duchess of Pershore's house was always a centre of Society, so she was able to write something called a gossip column, very lucrative apparently, on the strength of what she learned below-stairs.

But to return to Mipsie. One day, after reading an article in the *Queen* on the subject of American admiration of English Society, she bethought her of inserting an advertisement in a famous daily paper, graciously offering her help to American parents in launching their daughters. The response was overwhelming—so much so that she was able to pick and choose, and true to her ideals select only those families who loved their daughters so deeply that money was no object where their welfare was concerned. Her prospectus read as follows:

Minimum charge per season per daughter .	£500
With Court Presentation (this to include private dances, Ranelagh, Lords, etc. Court and special balls, Ascot, Box at Opera and personal contact with Royalty extra) . . .	£750

MARRIAGE TERMS.

English Duke	£2,000
Ditto Marquess or Earl	£1,500
Ditto, Viscount, Baron or Baronet . .	from £1,000
Foreign Royalty or title .	By arrangement
Financier . .	$2\frac{1}{2}$ per cent on Bridegroom's income

REDUCTIONS are allowed in the event of marriages with clergy, penniless Lieutenant, schoolmaster, country doctor, etc.

Mipsie had a very successful first season with this new venture, taking on two delightful girls at the full rate. Indeed, she was forced to charge more for one, pointing out to her parents that she had a slight squint and that marriage would therefore be more difficult to arrange, but her devoted father, Mr. Quiston B. Grape, was only too ready to pay the extra, and the result was a happy alliance with a new peer, in which Mipsie got the commission for a baron and also $2\frac{1}{2}$ per cent on his income, as she justly claimed that he would never have been given his title but for his generous contributions to party funds and that therefore he ranked as a financier. The other girl, pretty Mamie Druggett, was not quite so easy. The business started off badly by her having a great success at a dance with what she styled 'a real English Dooke'. Mipsie, who had been playing bridge downstairs and unfortunately lost, was too distracted to inquire his name, but cheered by the possibility of a good marriage for her young protégé, begged Mamie to invite him to dinner next day. When he arrived it transpired to be Oxo! Of course, with his brutal directness, he declared that nothing would induce him to handle anything sponsored by his former wife, and the disconsolate girl had to see her beau depart. Eventually she fell madly in love with a penniless young naval officer, which caused my sister much worry and many upsetting scenes with the girl, till it was suddenly discovered that that young man was heir to a baronetcy, so all was well and she was awarded her hard-earned commission.

But Fate seems to have decreed that nothing should succeed for long with my poor sister, and the following year saw the end of her valuable social work amongst American débutantes.

She had just married one girl to an Earl, after a slight unpleasantness with her father, who argued that the fee should be £1,500, whereas Mipsie charged £2,000 because he was a Duke's heir. Eventually it was amicably settled by Mipsie threatening to marry the bridegroom herself if she did not get her whole fee. She then had left only Alice McWhittle Potts, daughter of the biscuit king who could well afford more than £2,000. Mipsie looked everywhere for a foreign royalty but there were none available. Eventually, she went to the Balkans, where she had heard that it was easy to pick up Princes cheap at the time. Sure enough, she soon found a young man who declared that for £1,000 he could establish his claim as hereditary Prince of Sofa. Mipsie promised this sum, also marriage with a millionaire's daughter, on consideration of a reasonable income for herself after his wedding. All seemed well—Mr. Potts delighted at the prospect of a Prince, Alice enchanted with her bridegroom. Then a terrible thing happened. The Prince was unfortunately rather a heavy drinker, and when his prospective father-in-law arrived the day before the wedding, he was not entirely sober. Mr. Potts inquired: 'Are you His Highness?' The young man replied: 'I am no more Highness than you, sir, but Lady Millicent knows some old fool who will pay £1,000 for me to call myself Prince.'

The resulting scenes may be imagined! Mr. Potts was furious and said unforgivable things to Mipsie before he took his daughter away. The bridegroom seemed equally incensed and actually expected my sister to pay his debts in England. In the end, he accepted the cheque Addle gave him to return to his own country and the whole miserable affair was settled. But poor Mipsie's nerves were considerably shattered by the episode and I had to present her daughter Millie for her, as she said she felt, after her last experience, she could never touch a débutante again.

XVI

A THIRD DISILLUSIONMENT

AFTER the sadness of her second disillusionment (which word I always employ in Mipsie's case in preference to 'marriage') and her unlucky experiences in a wholly laudable attempt to earn her daily *brioche*, it is not surprising that my sister longed to start afresh, with 'a new country, new friends, new money,' as she expressed it. Accordingly she planned to go to America, in spite of the cruel treatment she had received from the U.S.A. through the person of Mr. McWhittle Potts. But forgiveness has ever been an inherent part of her sweet character, and she was greatly attracted by the stories her young débutantes had told her of that land of plenty of millionaires—stories which made her think that she might at last find a Utopia where there was not the endless stress and struggle for filthy lucre which lays waste our time elsewhere; it would just fall into her lap. She was fascinated too by the romantic tales the girls told her of their homes in New York and Baltimore—the picturesque gold dinner services, the old-world charm of rose diamonds round the porch.

She was just on the eve of departure, and Addle, who thoroughly approved this new step and had indeed even bought her ticket for her, was about to escort her to Liverpool 'so as to be sure she didn't get on the wrong ship and have to come back again,' as he jokingly put it, when Fate once more intervened.

At a soirée at the Russian Embassy she was presented

to Prince Fédor Ubetzkoi, already an old and sick man. These two qualities were quite enough to appeal to my sister's innate womanliness, and when she learnt that he was the ruler of Goulashia, with that beautiful little country solidly behind him—solid with platinum mines, that he was seventy-six and a widower, with a weak heart, her own heart contracted with pain at the thought of the journey she had so nearly taken. 'Do the work that's nearest' was a favourite motto of my beloved mother's, and Mipsie must have recollected it at this moment, for within a week she had cancelled all her plans and as Princess Fédor Ubetzkoi was journeying back with her husband to Ekaterinbog, the capital of Goulashia.

Here the first of her disappointments awaited her.

Fédor can hardly be blamed perhaps for his age, for that very senility which appealed to Mipsie so greatly, but he would have been well advised to have had some young attaché or A.D.C. always at hand to tell strangers what had apparently passed completely from his mind, that he had by a first marriage a daughter of forty, Irina, who ruled like a queen in Ekaterinbog, and a twenty-five year old son Michel, who would of course inherit Goulashia and every grain of platinum in the country.

However, Mipsie was never one to cry over spilt Bristol Milk, and she soon accepted the situation philosophically and looked around for where her next task lay. Immediately she saw her duty clear. Prince Fédor was obviously not long for this world; but Prince Michel was young—the future of Goulashia and everything in it was in his hands. My sister determined that she would join hands with him in this sacred trust.

She was abundantly rewarded. Michel became completely devoted to his stepmother, and for two happy years they were scarcely ever—indeed the maliciously-minded said never—apart. But Mipsie cared not a fig

PRINCE MICHEL UBETSKOI

for gossip and she and 'Mich' just laughed at court disapproval and Irina's frowns. (For some unaccountable reason the Princess seemed against my sister from the first.) They rode, danced and fished in the lake together. They indulged in revolver practice on the palace chickens, a special breed in which Princess Irina took great pride. She begged her father to intervene and he actually put his foot down and insisted that they practice on serfs instead. (Prince Fédor was a great admirer of England, and when he heard that pheasant shooting was a pastime of the landed gentry he determined to adopt it in his own country. Unfortunately, not being a good linguist, he interpreted the phrase as 'peasant shooting' and acted accordingly.) Above all, they took part in private theatricals.

All my family have inherited histrionic ability to a marked degree. My brother Crainy is known as Crambo to this day, so effective was he in dumb parts, while Mipsie was always inimitable as the black sheep when we sang the famous nursery rhyme to visitors. It happened that acting had also been a great tradition at Ekaterinbog Palace, where there was a beautiful little theatre, decorated in sky-blue plush and platinum, each *fauteuil* being fitted with a crystal carafe of vodka and a small revolver, in case a revolution should break out unexpectedly in the middle of a performance. So far, the court had only given the French classics, but Mipsie changed all that as she changed many things in Goulashia. She introduced light opera, musical comedy and even pantomime, playing the principal boy's role herself. To the amazed and scandalized palace set she tried to explain that it was 'an old English custom,' but they were, I fear, too rigid and prejudiced to appreciate this facet of British culture. She received, however, the whole-hearted support of the army, and especially of Prince Fédor's bodyguard, who made Mispie the toast of every regimental dinner, drinking her health in their own top boot and then throwing the boot on the fire, as was the Goulashian custom. The officer who could hop home after the festivities without toppling over was then supposed to win the lady. One day thirty officers hopped home successfully! Poor Mipsie, she never told me how she got out of that quandary, as State affairs kept her too busy to write for several weeks.

Meanwhile, like a snake in the grass, the storm clouds were brewing in Ekaterinbog which were shortly to undermine the silver lining of my sister's happiness.

XVII

REVOLUTION IN GOULASHIA

In my last chapter I told my dear readers how Mipsie introduced many things to her adopted country—good old English customs such as pantomime, brandy and soda, rubber hot-water bottles at the palace, to replace their primitive though picturesque platinum warming-pans, which she had sent home to England instead, as a keepsake. She also persuaded Prince Fédor to alter the New Year tradition of every man and woman saluting their own sex with three kisses, accompanied by the greeting 'St. Plasticine attend thee,' to the same delightful action applied to the opposite sex instead. It was a popular move with the more advanced Students' Party and with the army, but in the rigid Court circles it was considered an innovation. Other things seemed to Mipsie unjust and uncivilized and she threw all the weight of her husband and stepson into a gallant attempt to amend them. For instance, it was customary to pay honour only to unmarried women in Goulashia. On midsummer day the men would always present young girls with gifts, accompanied by a sprig of maidenhair fern, while the married women received nothing, and those who had had more than one husband were forced to shut themselves up all day with their blinds drawn. This struck my sister as positively cruel and while she was in Goulashia she did her utmost to establish the proper position of married women and special recognition of divorcées. In this she had Fédor's full support—indeed he was first attracted to Mipsie because of her late divorce, which he believed to be an integral part of the English Society he admired so greatly—and for Prince Michel of course she could do no wrong. But her stepdaughter Irina thought otherwise, and she, unfortunately, still held sway over a large portion of the population.

The first sign of trouble was a small bomb in Mipsie's muff which she suddenly discovered whilst attending Sunday service in the cathedral. She dropped it in the alms-box and thought no more of the matter. But two days later she found another concealed in a hat which came by post from Paris. It must be explained that in Goulashia revolutions were very frequent, and every peasant was taught to make bombs from childhood. A whole family used to sit round the fire in winter time, Mipsie told me, carving and painting with great skill, bombs of every shape and size. Luckily the Goulashians were very poor mechanics so it was rare for one actually to go off; still, it was a factor that had to be considered, and as chocolate-coated bombs began to appear in a full box of sweets ('my bon-bombs' Mipsie used laughingly to call them) and tiny white bombs in her sugar basin on her breakfast tray, it became necessary for her maid to sample everything first, in case of accidents.

On Easter Sunday, 1910, the storm burst. When Prince Fédor, in accord with an age-old custom, presented each of his bodyguard with a brightly-painted bad egg at the Easter Parade, the men one and all dashed the eggs to the ground, where they broke into a thousand chickens. The same day, slogans began to appear all over Ekaterinbog; '*Przmt copijk Britovzka bgowdl.*' 'Get rid of the British ——' Mipsie said I shouldn't understand the last word even if it were translated. To make things worse, Fédor's ninety-six-year-old mother, Princess Amnesia Ubekskoi, immediately moved back to the palace, saying that she had always been on the spot for every revolution and was not going to alter the habits of a lifetime. She was devoted to Princess Irina, and was consequently another thorn in Mipsie's all-too-tender side.

Even so, it is doubtful if my sister—absorbed in her delightful friendship with Prince Michel—realized fully the seriousness of the situation, until she learnt of the strikes in the platinum mines. Immediately she awoke to the danger that might befall Goulashia, should her staple industry be ruined. Mipsie herself had asked Fédor, on their marriage, for a block of platinum shares, 'so that she could share in the life-blood of her new country' as she beautifully expressed it. She knew, therefore, that the strikes could only bring disaster—bread famine for the people, dividend famine for herself. As ever with her, action followed knowledge.

The Goulashians are an intensely superstitious people, And especially do they revere their patron saint, St. Plasticine, who was actually a reigning prince in the fourteenth century, canonized on account of his liberality to the poor. He is depicted always in white, with flowing golden hair and beard, carrying a jewelled box containing roubles. Mipsie had the brilliant idea of donning her costume for Prince Charming in *Cinderella* and, accompanied by Michel, driving by sleigh round to the various mines, where inflammatory meetings were held most evenings. An arc light, attached to the horse's tail, shone full upon her as she made her stirring appeal, as from their patron saint. The effect was electrical. Some knelt, many wept, all went back to the mines. . . .

Thus did my sister persuade 90 per cent of the strikers to resume work. (What irony, as she said afterwards, that she should persuade men not to 'down tools' when two husbands had done so to her!) But at length there came a day when the welcome was so overpowering that the crowd came too close. One miner inadvertently knocked from Mipsie's hand the jewelled box, associated with the saint, which she always carried. It opened as it fell—and out of it poured sticks of grease-paint, mascara, yards of false hair. The next moment a foreman, his suspicions suddenly aroused, twitched away Mipsie's long golden beard—and a howl of fury went up from the mob: 'It's the English——' (again that word that I shouldn't understand.) Somehow, Michel got Mipsie away to safety, and the discovery was hushed up by all the miners concerned being sent to Siberia. My sister had saved the country—but at what a price! For in the emergency they were forced to abandon the sleigh which they had used throughout the tour—a sleigh in which the whole of the driver's seat had been filled almost to the brim with solid platinum nuggets.

XVIII

C'EST LA GUERRE!

SOON after the romantic happenings of the last chapter, when Mipsie saved Goulashia from the gory fangs of revolution, other troubles descended upon my poor sister which were to make her hate the very name of marriage. Chief among them was the engagement of her stepson, Prince Michel, and the end of the friendship which had perhaps been the happiest part of her life. 'Mich is going to marry that horrible little Xenia Nastikoff,' she wrote despairingly to me in 1911, 'and I, who love every inch of him, am thrust aside, without even a settlement to remember him by.' This tragic betrayal from one to whom she had indeed given amazing devotion for a stepmother, seemed to have the effect of drawing Mipsie closer to her husband, who was now a complete invalid, his mind wandering in a most distressing manner.

Talking of wandering minds recalls a cousin of my mother's, the fifth Duke of Brawling, whose senility took the form of making new and decidedly eccentric wills almost daily, witnessed only by his terrified servants (for he was a violent man). What was his widow's consternation to learn, when eventually the last will was read, that he had left his entire fortune to his horse! She afterwards had cause for rejoicing, however, for the horse soon died too and, having no heirs, the money returned to his benefactor's family, while no death duties were paid either by the horse or the Duchess, because it was found that there were no laws in England relating to death duties for horses.

Some remembrance of this story may have been in Mipsie's mind, however—possibly recalled by Princess Irina's strong resemblance to a horse—which induced her scarcely to leave Prince Fédor's side during the three long weary years which remained to her of his life. She was rewarded by finding herself, at his death in 1914, quite comfortably off, and for the first time able to afford little comforts that mean so much to a woman—an extra car or two, and more than just the one tiara. (Many a time during her hard life has she been reduced to a few bare evening gowns, scarcely enough to hold body and legs together.) She settled down very comfortably at Biarritz, where the simple seaside life appealed to her after the formal splendours of Ekaterinbog, and her colour, drained from her cheeks by Fédor's dimly lit sick-room, soon turned to a lovely peach bloom under the dazzling lights of the Casino.

My dear readers will guess what shattered that brief respite. War—which came with such appalling suddenness to us all. I myself shall never forget that terrible day, which was graven doubly on my heart by a small Bengers tragedy. A favourite sow of Addle's had just presented her boar with a fine litter of eight piglets. But some germ must have attacked the poor little things, for by the evening five of them had died. Next day my husband came to me with a look on his face which betokened bad news. 'What is it?' I asked in alarm. 'Is it the children——?' 'No, my dear,' he answered gravely. 'The rest of the litter has died and we are at war.'

But to return to Mipsie. Those who have appraised my sister's character through these pages will sense without any word of mine that her career was vivid in the extreme. Strange tales are told of her during those fearful years—how a German spy once lay under her bed, jotting down notes, for one whole night; how she was seen in Brussels on Armistice Day seated in a gun-carriage drawn entirely by Generals. It is said that one should only believe half that is told, so these rumours may be false. Though somebody once said of Mipsie that you can believe 150 per cent, double it, and then add the number you first thought of! It was some time before my sister found her real niche in the war, and though, like all of us, she threw herself into work from the start, her early efforts were somewhat unlucky. She began by working in the Censor Office, but left early in 1915 owing to a stupid misunderstanding on their part, so typical of official red tape.

There was a certain Parliamentary Under Secretary at that time—I will call him Lord X—who seemed indeed to have every qualification for success; youth, good looks, money, brains, He was already forecast for a ministerial post in Government circles. Mipsie had met him several times and formed the same high opinion of him. What was her disappointment therefore to have a letter pass through her hands at the Censor Office from Lord X to a young V.A.D. in France, containing an offer of marriage. The girl was a complete nobody, with, obviously, none of the qualities suited to the wife of a coming man, who needed some one of intelligence and social brilliance —such as, for instance, Mipsie's delightful daughter Millie, aged twenty-four, who was working then at the Admiralty. My sister could not bear to think that a great career, possibly a future Prime Minister, might be ruined by the wrong marriage, so she deleted the proposal, and cleverly contrived to censor the letters that followed, which demanded, naturally, why the girl had never replied to his first offer. Meanwhile, Mipsie arranged that Lord

X and Millie should see plenty of each other, and I am convinced—suffering from pique and loneliness as he was—that another week would have seen the young couple happily engaged, when unfortunately the V.A.D. was taken ill and invalided home. The whole facts of the censored letters somehow came out and were unluckily attributed to Mipsie, who was requested to resign from the Censor Office in consequence.

She left with a sick heart, reflecting, as many great men must have reflected in the past, when their noble plans for their country's welfare had gone astray, how hard is Britannia's shield, how cruelly sharp her spear.

XIX

GREAT DEEDS IN THE GREAT WAR

I WISH I could say that my own life during the great war had been thrilling and romantic, as Mipsie's was, but candour compels me to admit that mine was the part of a very humble (except in birth) cog. There were, of course, my knitting parties at Bengers, where, being of an inventive turn of mind, I enjoyed spurring my workers on to new creations, such as knitted pyjamas for hospital patients, knitted scarlet bands for staff hats, etc. I still think that almost every manufacturing shortage could have been bridged by voluntary knitwork, but the powers that be usually lack my vision, I find. I actually knitted one whole field-gun cover in waterproof wool myself, and got it sent out as a sample to Havre, where the English authorities saw fit to despise it, but the more imaginative French used it for years, I am told, in connexion with catching langoustes, so my labours were not in vain. Another invention of mine was dog-basket cookery, on the hay-box cooking theory, only employing the natural warmth of a dog's body to heat a specially-shaped dish, concealed beneath a cushion. It only failed because the dogs used in experiments *would* 'make their bed', discover the food and then eat it. Apart from these homely occupations I cannot boast of any excitements at Bengers, and it is not surprising that Mipsie, who took sanctuary with us after her shocking treatment from the Censor Office, soon felt a longing for a more vital and active life. She did splendid work going round to recruiting meetings with

Addle, where her winning ways brought many a volunteer to the colours, but my husband found one day that she was giving all the recruits the traditional shilling encased in little lockets, showing the actual king's head on one side and her own likeness on the other. Addle is perhaps on the conventional side, and he considered this slight infringement of regulations ill-advised, and told Mipsie so. After that her enthusiasm seemed to wane, and she appeared restless. I encouraged her to help our working parties by reading out to us, but I must confess that her choice of books was not always suitable for village people.

One day her pent-up feelings broke out, after a specially long afternoon's work. Throwing the copy of *Three Weeks* which she had been reading across the room, she suddenly exclaimed: 'Blanchie, I can't go on here any longer. I'm going to France, or anyway to London. I must get closer to our men.' Who shall blame her for following the dictates of her glowing heart?

There was at that time a great appeal for châteaux and hotels well behind the firing lines to be offered as convalescent homes to relieve the hospitals. Mipsie immediately offered the beautiful château of her friend, the Duc D'Aperitif, who was, of course, fighting, so she took his consent for granted, and was soon installed there, making all arrangements for staff and seventy beds for French officers. What was her surprise and dismay when a car drove up to the château one day, containing—the Duchesse D'Aperitif! The Duc in his friendship with my sister had never mentioned that he was married, so she can hardly be blamed for acting in ignorance of the fact, but unfortunately that did not help matters with his wife, who for some unknown reason seemed incensed at Mipsie running a convalescent home at the château, when she had (so she said!) returned with the express purpose of doing so herself. However, possession is nine-tenths of the law, so, after a very exhausting half-hour for my poor sister, the Duchesse left, threatening to open a home at the large, and before the war very fashionable, Hôtel D'Angleterre at Coquille Plage *one mile away*! The small-mindedness of some women is truly amazing. As Mipsie said, when all that mattered was the wounded soldiers, how any one could argue about such trivial things as property just passed belief, but the fact remains that the Duchesse did set up what amounted to a rival convalescent home, and what is worse, tried by every means in her power to make it a greater success than the Château D'Aperitif, where poor Mipsie had to labour under many disadvantages—out-of-date equipment, shortage of bathrooms and so on; whereas the Hôtel D'Angleterre was, of course, completely up-to-date in every way. My sister sent down almost daily complaints and demands for new domestic utensils. They were completely ignored. In self-defence Mipsie had then to ignore the Duchesse's orders requisitioning the garden produce from the château. This rivalry became known in the village as *la bataille de 'rouge et noir,'* because the Duchesse always appeared in smartest black, while Mipsie dressed very simply in pure white chiffon, her only colouring being a red cross embroidered in tiny garnets on her snowy head-handkerchief, and a bright scarlet arm-band bearing the letter B and the Briskett coronet in semi-precious stones. (For with wonderful loyalty to her first husband, she always returns, after each marriage, to the rank and title of an English Duchess.) The bitter struggle continued for four months, then suddenly, the Duc D'Aperitif appeared one day and confronted Mipsie in her office in the Duchesse's boudoir. He told her that she would have to go. That his wife insisted, and the law was, unfortunately, on her side. Mipsie's eyes blazed at this miscarriage of justice. 'If I go,' she told him, 'I take my patients with me.'

And that is exactly what happened. One week later my sister left the château with sixty-seven officers—unfortunately three were too ill to travel—and shook the dust of Coquille Plage off her feet for ever. It is not the first time that a worth while and noble work has been ruined by a woman's petty jealousy, no doubt, but it sickened my sister of war service to such an extent that she spent the following few weeks in sick leave, with her patients. Then the old, brave Mipsie returned to her real character and she threw her energies into the selfless struggle once again.

XX

HOW MIPSIE WON THE WAR AND LOST THE PEACE

It was not until early in 1917 that Mipsie found her real métier in the great war, though she accomplished many wonderful things during the previous year, especially in liaison work, establishing a depot for Regimental Pets (though she was always the chief pet, as some admirer said), and as a voluntary inspector of Staff tennis courts. This last involved touring round the various H.Q's, often in great personal danger from her car skidding in ruts, and playing experimental games with the officers. Sometimes, of course, bad weather would preclude outdoor sports, so Mipsie would be the guest of Army Headquarters for a few days, and in that way she grew to know many of their needs; she often says that her Base memories would fill a book. It was these experiences that led her to open her famous Milli-Baba Café in Amiens. She realized that man's chief want in that grim and arid war was glamour—and she gave it to them with both hands.

Her first step, when she had found the right place—an enormous, almost empty wine cellar, which she and a few devoted helpers got completely clear in no time, was to appeal through the British Press for what she needed to give the desired atmosphere of an Eastern café. As always with Mipsie, the response was magnificent. She asked for beads—every jewel-box in the *beau monde* was opened to send her amber, lapis lazuli, cornelian, jade. . . . She wanted palms—there was not a conservatory in the stately homes of England that did not yield her of its best. Persian rugs, flowing draperies, almost too many brass gongs (people were particularly generous with Benares ware) poured into her depot at our London home in Eaton Square, and were somehow or other got out to France by my clever sister.

The opening of the Milli-Baba Café was almost as brilliant as a peace-time function. The waitresses, who were all dressed as houris, were drawn from the cream of Debrett (for it is one of Mipsie's great boasts that she has never been associated with the *demi-monde*—indeed, as she has frequently remarked, half of anything is too little.) So dukes and marquesses daughters handed round sandwiches which their mothers had cut up, and in some cases their grandmothers washed the plates behind a screen. Mipsie herself, dressed with war-time simplicity as the Queen of Sheba, dispensed champagne from earthenware ewers. It was all very homely and delightful.

Such was the popularity of the café, however, that she was forced, after a fortnight, to close it for one whole week-end, so that she and her staff could collect and restring the beads which the waitresses had worn and mend the rents in their *yashmaks*. It was then that they discovered a Quartermaster fast asleep in a large Benares pot which had been used as an ash-tray. He had been there since the opening. This decided Mipsie to make the Milli-Baba more exclusive, so that such incidents should not be repeated. Consequently she was compelled to raise her prices considerably, and this continued throughout the war, the popularity and the tariff rising above each other in a splendid spiral. There were some maliciously-minded persons who hinted that Mipsie was making 'a good thing' out of the venture and robbing our fighting men. I hope they may feel ashamed when they read the following facts.

We all remember the terrible time in the Spring of 1918 when the advancing Germans so nearly captured Amiens. Then suddenly there came a check—a check which proved the first stepping-stone to our final victory. It was not till after the armistice that I was shown a letter, which somehow had come into British hands, written by a high-up officer in the German army to his wife. In it he said that from all he heard about Amiens, it would be a bad thing for them if they captured it, as if the Duchess of Briskett was still there, Germany would have to *pay too dear for victory*. Some say that the words were meant in joke, but in my opinion it is clear that, in fact, my dear sister was instrumental, if not actually responsible, for *winning the great war*.

But where others receive high honours, pensions and grants, Mipsie's sole reward was the consciousness of a job well done, and what small profits, amounting to a few thousand francs (or pounds, I forget which) she had made out of the Milli-Baba—money which was soon to save her from complete ruin, as my dear readers will hear.

One day Addle and I were quietly sitting at Bengers, he going over pig notes, I endeavouring to use up some tarred twine which I had had for knitted sou-westers (a little war wrinkle of my own) by crocheting a jumper for Margaret, then an adorable little ruby-faced imp of six, when Mipsie burst into the room, with tears the size of her pearls (almost) coursing down her cheeks. 'Blanche,' she said wildly, 'the Russian revolution has spread to Goulashia. They have imported bombs that really go off. The palace is destroyed, Mich has fled, and I——' She staggered to a chair. 'My money is worth nothing.' I thought she was going to faint, and told Addle, who was standing sympathetically by, keeping only one finger on a design for pig-feeders, to ring for brandy, but when it came she seemed to rally as she helped herself to a tumbler full. 'It's the shock,' she apologized with her winsome smile, as she drained it.

'Dearest Mipsie,' I told her, 'you will surmount this as you have surmounted other troubles. Meanwhile you will, of course, look on Bengers as your home.'

Somewhat to my surprise, for he is very moderate as regards alcohol, my husband also poured himself out a tumbler of brandy and quickly drank it. 'I have had a shock, too,' he explained, catching my questioning eye. I think that incident shows the amazing devotion Mipsie inspires in all, that Addle, who is by no means emotional, could thus feel her troubles as his own.

XXI

MILLICENT

I FEEL that I should really apologize to my dear readers for this chapter, because it is largely about myself, which is a sad come-down from the colourful details of my beautiful sister's life.

After the terrible news of the revolution in her late husband's country and her own bankruptcy in consequence, Mipsie had once more to face the grim phantom of starvation—or starvation only slightly removed by the £3,000 a year allowed her by Oxo. Accordingly, she was forced to tackle yet again the problem of earning her living. She decided to open a hat shop.

She had found a charming little house in the depths of Mayfair, with a shop on the ground floor. The only difficulty was the price, which was high. But here she was helped by her new son-in-law, Sir Basil Warpe, whose engagement to her only daughter Millie Mipsie had bitterly opposed at first (he had gained his fortune and title from coco-nut matting, which is indeed a terrible thought in connexion with a duke's daughter.) But when my sister had seen him and learnt how kind and generous he was—he agreed to finance the whole of her new venture—she realized instantly that he was one of Nature's Gentlemen, and that solid worth was better than blue blood. The happy pair were married in the Spring of 1919, and a month later Mipsie opened her new shop under her own name of 'Millicent'.

For a while I saw little of her. She was frantically

busy, working day and night, she told me, to make a success. Then suddenly I got a wire from her: 'Must go to the Grand Prix to see the fashions. Can you keep an eye on the shop.' Thus began my own career in trade.

It wasn't until the following winter that I turned to designing millinery myself. The reason was that the stock was getting low, Mipsie having been away in Paris more and more, seeking the right models. (She has such a high standard.) One day I happened to bring up to London for re-covering an old red silk lamp-shade, and to leave it carelessly on the counter. To my surprise, a customer (an old friend of mine, Lady de Rusk, who is rather short-sighted) took it up quite naturally and tried it on, saying: 'This is nice and light to wear. I hate heavy hats. How do I look, Blanche?' In a flash I had draped a veil over the top and a feather round the rim. 'Connie', I told her, 'it's your hat.' She bought it!

That night I could hardly sleep for excitement and making plans for the future. I have always had rather original ideas, many of which I have passed on through these pages, so it may be imagined with what joy I entered, during the coming weeks, into the new and thrilling sphere of a creative artist. Scraps of lace from my piece drawer, peacock's feathers, fir-cones, old Shetland shawls dyed and stretched over wire frames, worn bedroom rugs, the best parts cut out and used in toques—all these contributed to what I could truthfully call 'original models'. Some, of course, were more successful than others. Before I learnt that feathers must be baked before use, I made one customer a lovely Ascot hat from one of our White Wyandottes, which she brought back to me in a condition which demanded, sad to say, its instant destruction. Another hat, with a pretty design in fish-bones sewn on to velvet ribbon with raffia, was returned and I had to refund the cost price, because a cat had eaten a large part of the crown. On the other hand I had my successes, my real triumph being when I was asked to design the millinery for a whole West End theatrical production—a play called *The Cranks*. How proud I felt at seeing Mipsie's name on the programme which they sent me—alas, I did not see the play. My work was keeping me away from home more than I really liked, and though Addle never complained, I sensed that he felt it, so made a point of getting back to Bengers directly the shop shut.

After that success came sudden disaster. A charming model I had made of tree bark, painted in gay scarlet enamel unfortunately melted in a hot room and stuck fast to its owner's hair, most of which she had to have cut off in consequence. She brought an action against 'Millicent' and was awarded damages. I insisted, against Mipsie's protests (she had to return to England for the case of course) in paying these myself, as it was my fault, and then urged her to go at once, as she had planned, to Cannes, where she said the sea air always gave her inspiration. It meant my remaining in London instead of going to Scotland with Addle, but that couldn't be helped.

Two days after she had departed an extraordinary thing happened. A little elderly man, with a parchment yellow face and the air of a lawyer, suddenly appeared in the shop one day and asked to buy the business. He was acting for an interested party, he said. I cabled to Mipsie who wired back asking £14,000—just double what she had paid for it, but after all there was now the goodwill, which amounted to quite a lot, for the notoriety of the case had filled the shop. I communicated the price to the agent, who accepted it instantly, without one quibble. 'Millicent' was sold!

Now comes the strange part. I was resting on my bed

(for truth to tell I had found the almost daily visits to town decidedly tiring) one day during the next week, thinking how brilliant Mipsie was to have made 100 per cent profit in so short a time, when I heard voices on the terrace. What was my astonishment, on looking from my window, to see Addle in close conversation with— my little parchment lawyer! When I got downstairs, my husband was alone in the library, doing his Press-cutting book and humming contentedly to himself. I told him what I had seen.

'Nonsense, my dear,' he answered to my amazement, 'you must have been dreaming. I've been here the whole afternoon. You're over-tired, that's what it is, but Scotland will soon put you right.'

Which it did. But I ask my dear readers, can any of you explain the reason for that extraordinary hallucination?

XXII

MELISANDE

BRIEF though it was, Mipsie's experience in trade as 'Millicent' served only to inspire her further. This time she decided that a dressmaking business would give more scope to her genius. 'What is a hat?' she said, whilst discussing the matter with me. 'A few flowers or feathers, worth twenty guineas at the most. But a lovely gown has no limit, either in imagination or price.'

Once again the right premises were her chief difficulty, for she had only the £14,000 she had made out of the sale of her hat shop, since when relations had been somewhat strained between her and her son-in-law, Sir Basil Warpe (he had some absurd idea that she should have repaid him his original capital), so she felt it would be unwise, or worse still, useless, to approach him for more funds. However, money has never really worried my light-hearted sister. 'Where there's a bill there's a way,' she often says laughingly. The right place must be found and the money for it would somehow follow.

We were in deserted Chine House—the Briskett's London home—one day, going through some drawers of family lace which she thought might be useful, when a sudden idea occurred to her. 'Blanchie,' she said excitedly, 'why shouldn't I open my dress shop here? Just think of the models parading down the great staircase—it would be wonderful!' 'It certainly would, darling,' I remember saying dubiously, 'but what would Oxo say?' Mipsie reflected, then dimpled. 'We wouldn't tell him,' she said. 'He is always in Scotland now and hardly ever comes south.' At that moment the door opened and a tall, rather handsome girl entered the room. 'Will you please tell me what you are doing here?' asked Mipsie coldly. 'I am the Duchess of Briskett.' To our astonishment the girl replied: '*So am I*'! It appears that Oxo, in a thoroughly deceitful manner, had married again without a word to his former wife.

Eventually Mipsie took a shop in Bond Street at a high rent, and also spent a large sum on its re-decoration. Next she set about designing the models, and she appeared at Bengers one day laden with bales of lovely material and demanding some one to drape! We tried to persuade Addle—for I was unfortunately too plump—to help the good cause, but even though we allowed him to read his favourite book on pig-keeping while Mipsie pinned chiffon and velvet on him for one whole evening, he did not really enter into the fun somehow. But the second footman, Mipsie discovered, had an excellent figure and was very obliging and patient, besides being so good looking that Mipsie said his face alone immediately gave her ideas.

Eventually all her models were ready and Maison Melisande opened, with instantaneous success. Mipsie was clever enough to realize that with all the first-class Paris firms as competitors she must offer other attractions to clients beyond mere clothes. So the staff included a fortune teller, a racing tipster, and a private detective whose services were at the disposal of customers with accounts of £1,000 a year or over who were anxious to gain information about their husbands or friends. Then there were what Mipsie called her 'Petites Vignettes'. With brilliant psychological insight she realized that every woman loved to see herself as a different type. So

MIPSIE WITH HER FIRST HUSBAND, ‘OXO’ BRISKETT

for a few guineas a royalty could contemplate herself in the mirror as a midinette, a governess could look at her image dressed as Madame Dubarry, a welfare worker could revel in the feeling that she was Cleopatra. It was astonishing how popular these little 'let's pretend' scenes were. But most successful of all were Maison Melisande's Dress Parades for Husbands, which were arranged as follows: A customer would perhaps like a dress she had seen on an ordinary day. If she could afford it, well and good, if not she would specify that it should be shown to her husband (at an increased price). This simple scheme pleased both parties. The wives got more clothes and the husbands enjoyed the parades, which were exclusively for men, so greatly that they did not grudge the money for their wife's gown. And gradually Mipsie extended the facilities to include a telephone for every customer, so that a busy man could continue to conduct business in delightful surroundings. But this very consideration for her clients led to more misfortune.

The switchboard for the various telephones was, of course, a complicated one. So Mipsie, who never considers herself too grand for any menial job, always insisted on taking over the operator's work during the Husband's Dress Parades, so as to be certain that efficient service was given. In this way it was inevitable that she should glean a good deal of City information, which she would have been scarcely human if she had not used to her own advantage. Unluckily, however, a big deal which she made in Ubango shares seemed to upset a certain financier, who was a regular customer of Maison Melisande's. He dared to accuse my sister of tapping what he considered should have been treated as a private line. The dispute became publicised, which led to the ground landlord of the shop—a strict Methodist—to pay a visit of inspection to the establishment. He could not have come on a more unfortunate day. He arrived towards the end of a Husbands' Parade and discovered a Cabinet Minister dancing the tango with one model, while a well-known sporting peer was telephoning to his bookmaker, with another model holding the telephone on his knee. His impressions were worsened by several empty champagne bottles—used for local colour, Mipsie said—placed about the showroom. He gave my sister notice on the spot, and when she pointed out the enormous sum she had spent on re-decoration, he threatened a public inquiry into the conduct of the shop should she attempt to claim one penny. She was thrown out of Bond Street, a pauper—save for £3,000 a year and a small, pathetically small, fortune in Ubangos.

XXIII

AMERICA

ALL through history we read of good women who suddenly realize the hollow mockery of the world and yearn only to escape to some sequestered spot, away from it all. Some have entered convents; others have found solace in the simple countryside. Mipsie sought sanctuary in New York.

She was too sick at heart even to face the winding-up of Maison Melisande, so I undertook the business for her, though the whole thing was very strange to me. There were some items in the schedule of assets which I had *no idea* were needed in a dressmaker's establishment. However, it was all done at last, and Addle took me to Brighton for a week's change, which was very refreshing. Indeed, Mipsie's departure, which must have depressed him as much as it did all of us—for it is like the sun ceasing to shine when my radiant sister goes away—brought out all my husband's bravery and cheerfulness under adversity. The evening she sailed he seemed positively merry, and insisted on taking me to dine in a restaurant, then to a musical comedy and finally to supper at the Savoy—an evening packed with new experiences which I must admit I thoroughly enjoyed, though I felt decidedly fast, having supper with a man!

I was soon heartened by hearing from Mipsie that she was very happy and had already plunged into hard work—as always with her the sweet and womanly work of helping others—she was lending her face to encourage humanity by means of advertisement campaigns.

Her approach to the subject was, as usual, practical and businesslike in the extreme. She charged according to rank. So much to be photographed as a baronet's wife and earl's daughter—Lady Millicent Standing. A higher rate for her picture as the Duchess of Briskett, and more still as Princess Fédor Ubetskoi—for to her sorrow she found that the American public, though delightful, were sufficiently uncultured to place a foreign royalty above an English duchess.

Needless to say, that country of big business was not slow to take advantage of such opportunities, and during the following year—1924—Mipsie was in constant demand. Gallantly she threw aside all personal feelings, and with splendid impartiality she appeared both for flesh reducing pills and fattening tonics, and lent her support to every political party that was prepared to assess it at its real value. She featured in brilliant social functions wearing Fifth Avenue's finest diamonds, and at revivalist mass meetings, where she was once paid as much as $1,000 for one hallelujah. There were minor misfortunes of course, such as the time when she caught a bad chill advertising waterproof underwear at Niagra Falls (though she received substantial compensation when she threatened, in the interests of the public, to disclose the fallibility of the goods, as well as her fee for advertising them, so all ended well). There was also an amusing episode when she was engaged to speak to the Volstead Society in praise of prohibition and to an assembly of hotel proprietors advertising fifty ways of serving up whisky in disguise during the same evening. *She mixed the talks up* and showed the prohibitionists how spirits can be sent up in invalid cups, or sucked through a straw from an ice-cream soda glass with a false bottom, and so forth. But this proved one of her most successful demonstrations, as all the prohibitionists crowded round her and placed a record number of orders for her exhibits.

Eventually her work grew to such an extent that she was forced to combine several advertisements in one in order to conserve her strength. For example, she might be photographed in a bathing suit, contemplating a waffle with a dazzling smile. Thus, in one picture, she would be advertising the bathing gown in, say, a New York paper as Duchess of Briskett, a brand of maple syrup for a Chicago firm and forwarding a dentifrice campaign in California. It was a brilliantly daring idea, for of course each firm believed that they had exclusive rights of the picture. But faith can move mountains, we have all been brought up to believe, and as Mipsie said—if mountains, why not managing directors? Her theory was soon put to the test.

One day, early in 1925, she received a wire from the chairman of Block's Skin Bleaching Cream: 'Have just seen our picture of you employed by Kuddly Crisps Cereals. Please report to our New York office immediately.' Next morning, dressed in pearly grey which accentuated the whiteness of her face, with two tears shining like drops of glycerine on her cheeks, she entered the office of—her future husband!

'Mr. Block,' she said, 'no American citizen can possibly understand the agony of body and soul a British aristocrat suffers in work of this kind. If I am to preserve my health for the Stars and Stripes, you must——' but she got no further. In two steps Mr. Block was by her side, holding her hands in a warm grip.

'Lady,' he said (or it may have been 'baby'—Mipsie was never quite sure) 'I have been in the advertising world for twenty years—I am the author of seventeen books on the subject, including *Dandy Ads, Sex in Salesmanship* and *Psycho-Suckers*, and listen, Baby' (or possibly 'lady') 'I hand it to you that you're the greatest business woman I have ever met. What will you take to come into partnership with me?'

Well, my dear readers know how it all ended. That evening Mr. Block arrived to take Mipsie out to dinner pushing before him a life-sized silver coffin entirely filled with orchids. (He was just like a schoolboy in his jokes.) 'The old Julius Block is dead,' he announced. 'Since I saw you a new man has been born.' Later he confided to her his hopes and aspirations—to graduate from a millionaire to a multi-millionaire, to have his solid lapis swimming pool at his beloved little twenty-roomed cottage 'Gnomeshome' fitted with a gold diving-board, and so on. As he told her in his simple way some of these boyish ideals, Mipsie suddenly realized that a miracle had happened.

She knew that she loved again.

XXIV

THE LAST TRAGEDY

MIPSIE was married to Julius Keatings Block in the summer of 1925, and took up residence with her fourth husband partly at his Fifth Avenue apartment and partly at his beautiful Long Island cottage, Gnomeshome. As I said in my last chapter Julius was, although the wrong side of fifty and weighing over seventeen stone, just one big Peter Pan. He gloried in fairies and all the whimsies of elf-land till his dying day. But he was also a hard-headed and brilliant business man with an American's true flair for advertisement, so his house, which he designed himself, was an interesting combination of his varied qualities. As its name suggests it was a real home for gnomes. Every doorway was flanked by two gnomes who opened the door directly a visitor stepped on a mechanical contrivance beneath the mat. In the garden a small army of gnomes fishing round the lake would draw up, on pressing a button in their little chests, a pot of Block's Skin Bleaching Cream. Delightful little embossed silver gnomes sat athwart the bathroom taps, the turning on of which made the gnomes open their mouths and discourse on the virtues of a white skin. There was even a metrognome on the piano, to beat time with his tiny hand, while the piano seat was an exquisite orange toadstool, carried out in velvet broché with the spots in mother-of-pearl.

Like every foreigner whose heart is in the right place, Julius cherished a deep admiration for England and especially for the British aristocracy. So on his marriage, as a compliment to Mipsie, he had coronets fitted on every gnome's head, the coats of arms of all her family, including her three previous husbands, hand-painted on satin panels round the dining-room, and installed a picturesque half-timbered bar, over which he presided himself, dressed in hunting-pink and dispensing cocktails in gold tankards.

There was something irresistibly cosy and soothing about the atmosphere of this unusual house, Mipsie said. A little vulgar by our standards perhaps, but it comforted her to think of the wealth of imagination—and dollars—which had contributed to the home of this gay, puck-like, yet completely well-bank-balanced man. Nevertheless, despite their happiness, troubles lay ahead.

It was about a year after their marriage that Mipsie began to realize that her husband had some reason to fear for his life. Small things—finding a bill for a bullet-proof summer-house, seeing him slip a miniature machine-gun into his golf-bag—told the tale. Once he was sent a poisoned gnome through the post. Then came the terrible day when she was motoring out of New York and, on a lonely stretch of road, her car was held up by three men. One gagged the chauffeur, another drugged her maid, and threw them both out into the roadway. Then the three men took possession of the car with my poor sister in it. She was kidnapped.

They seemed to have no hesitation in telling her the whole story. Apparently Julius Block, besides being Skin Bleaching King, also made a considerable fortune on the side through the sale of illicit liquor. This he had only done since his marriage to Mispie, so as to give her the little extra comforts a cultured woman needs, and he lived in terror of New York and Long Island society and his brother Elks, finding out his guilty secret. The intention of the gangsters was therefore to hold Mipsie as a prisoner, until ransomed by her husband, with the threat of exposure as an additional lever to the unfortunate Julius. Mipsie, with her acute brain, took in the situation in a flash. 'Leave it all to me,' she told her kidnappers.

My sister has been bitterly criticized for her behaviour at that time. It was said—when the whole story unluckily came out later—that she had collaborated with her captors by writing pleading letters to her husband daily, telling him of her miseries and begging him to send more, and still more money, which she then, by arrangement, halved with the gangsters. If they objected she refused to write another letter. But they did not object. They appreciated a business woman's acumen and were glad, before they released her, to claim only half of the £800,000 which was eventually wrung from her distracted husband. It is said that they even offered her a permanent partnership, so great was their admiration.

But I know the true story, as Mipsie told it to me. She was, she said, deeply shocked to discover that Julius drew money from illegal sources and she thought the only solution was 'to teach him a lesson.' Yet at the same time she hated the idea of his parting with so large a slice of his precious fortune, so cleverly contrived to keep half of it 'in the family.' Thus, her seeming disloyalty to her husband was in reality a splendid wifely devotion.

Alas, their happiness of reunion was short-lived. Soon came the great slump, and on top an unpredictable bit of ill fortune. The fashion for sun-bathing suddenly came in. The bottom dropped out of white skins—and of Block's Skin Bleaching Cream. For a time they tried desperately to stem the tide by paying Hollywood beauties to keep white, commissioning Press articles on the vulgarity of tanned skin, even contemplating taking some of America's Society leaders into safe custody for a time.

The last was Mipsie's idea. 'Let's put the snatch on a Vanderbilt,' she said. She picked up a lot of quaint *patois* in the States.

But it was all useless. One day news reached Julius that sun-tanned arms had been seen at the English Court. 'It is the end,' he groaned. He felt he could not face telling Mipsie the tragic news. They found him in his office later—shot through the head.

At his funeral thirty-six cars carried the flowers alone—many in the form of gigantic toadstools. There was a purple pall embroidered with a huge gnome in golden sequins. Yet even that, as a friend said, had its tragic side. In his hey-day the sequins would have been of solid gold.

XXV

DECORATIVE INTERLUDE

As she journeyed back to England, utterly alone on the *Aquitania*, Mipsie's sad thoughts had once more to turn to the question of her living—what to embark on and who was to finance it, for she was now decidedly past her first youth and it came hard to contemplate, after so many years in business, using her own capital. Still, as she so romantically put it: 'If real gilt-edged beauty is a woman's stock the market will never be dull.' And this dictum was soon proved.

She had, of course, instantly attracted attention and admiration on board ship, partly by reason of her looks and partly by her deep mourning, unrelieved by any jewels except a triple rope of pearls, a solitary solitaire ring, a few simple diamond bracelets and a large sobbing gnome in brilliants, the tears being executed in sapphires, which was her husband's last commission to his jewellers before taking his life. It was a touching memento of him which she was proud to wear and only sold when she reached England because she was, unfortunately, allergic to gnomes, especially on the person. But to return to the *Aquitania*.

A certain millionaire peer, who I will call Lord B, was also crossing to England, and was just the type of financier Mipsie was seeking. A chance remark of his, when she had made some comment on the decoration of the ball-room: 'But you are the chief decorator, Lady Millicent,' gave her an idea. She had always loved the home beautiful. Why not consecrate her talents to the décor profitable? Lord B seemed only too anxious to finance her. By the end of the voyage he had reached his goal and Mipsie knew that her future was assured.

She started 'Millicent Briskett' at a time when there was still the craze for modern furniture and decoration. With her usual thoroughness Mipsie threw herself into the trend, and indeed added several new ideas herself. Many will remember her drainpipe tables and her wire-netting sofas, which made a lasting impression on all who encountered them. 'Strip, strip and strip again—and then begin constructive work,' was her motto. She held that humanity, silted up by ennui, needed everything new to refresh its jaded palate. So she designed glass tables and wooden tumblers, tea-sets of metal and spoons and forks of china. It was all rather beyond my humble brain and Addle became quite angry when I let Mipsie redecorate his study as a surprise after a fishing holiday. He said he 'wouldn't have his house turned into a damned operating theatre.' So sadly I sent everything back and replaced the old stag's heads (Mipsie had installed chromium cats) and Morris wall-paper. One or two other clients did the same, I believe, and it was most unfortunate that Lord de Quinsy's little daughter fell down in a kind of fit on seeing the nursery which Mipsie had designed for her for the first time. The indisposition was only a coincidence, of course, but it created a bad impression.

Luckily, however, my sister's guardian angel never quite deserts her and at about this time her own taste underwent a drastic change and swung right over to the antique. She held that humanity, instinctively ruled by fear, clung to established forms. From then on she sought only the mellowed, the time-worn, the faded and the worm-eaten. She delighted especially in finding for her American clients what she well knew, from marriage to

Julius, they would most appreciate, 'a bit of olde England.' No trouble was too great for the discovery of these precious relics. She would send her scouts into every little inn and lonely farmhouse in the country, while she sat at the end of a telephone at Claridge's, scarcely daring to move, lest one of them should telephone with news of a new purchase. She was very clever too in converting unusual objects for domestic use. A gibbet for a lamp standard, an old mill-stone for a fender stool, bag-pipes for cushions and so forth.

From 1934–1938 her business was most successful and I was beginning to hope that her luck had turned and her disasters were all behind her. Alas, how wrong I was.

She dealt, naturally, in pictures as well as furniture, though she was always a little diffident about these, feeling a lack of the highest expertise. (Tiresome little things such as Van Eyck and Van Dyck having names so similar confused her.) Always over-conscientious, she would insist on going to see any picture purchased from her hung, so as to be certain it was well placed. Often she would take it back to re-frame.

Suddenly a client who had just returned from America startled her by saying that he had seen the Vermeer which he had bought from 'Millicent Briskett' in a private house in Washington. Its owner had purchased it from Mipsie too, and both clients had paid the price of an original Vermeer. Unfortunately the story got about, and in less than a month twelve other clients had had their pictures, which they bought as old masters, pronounced as fakes by experts. All had let the canvases be sent back to Mipsie for re-framing.

My sister was appalled. Could she conceivably have mixed the pictures up while they were at the shop? It was not an impossibility, for she was always adorably vague. She could only plead her ignorance and beg, with many tears, her clients' forgiveness. She visited each one in turn and all agreed not to prosecute—except one. He was a chartered accountant. 'No figure means anything to me except on paper,' he told Mipsie bluntly. He brought, in 1939, an action against her for fraud.

How my dear sister, with her delicate sensitiveness and frail finances, would ever have stood the case I know not. I was already considering selling my tiara, after having it copied (Mipsie knew all about having copies made to order—so clever of her) so that Addle need not know, when the last great calamity broke upon us all on that fatal September day. The chartered accountant, thank Heaven, agreed to drop the case and Mipsie was saved. We must all remember that Hitler did that one good thing in his life.

XXVI

LIFE GOES ON

THE outbreak of the European war found my sister, in spite of the terrible blows which Fate had dealt her, still gallantly carrying on—'faint yet persuing', 'bloody but unbowed.'

Her first act, in accord with her life-long patriotism, was to offer her little house in Mayfair to the Government at a ridiculously small rent (it was just crass stupidity that made them disregard the offer) and to take a delightful small manor house in Buckinghamshire instead. Here she did splendid work entertaining tired ministers and officers of high rank but low powers of resistance, for charming and refreshing week-ends. Her altruistic work was brought to a sudden end by the warning of no less than seven evacuees! Mipsie felt that the peaceful atmosphere so sorely needed by war workers would be shattered, so quickly sub-let the house. Luckily, her notorious bad memory stood her in good stead at this juncture; she completely forgot to mention the evacuees, so let the manor at a substantial profit, which came in very handy on her return to London, where she felt that to live at a first-class hotel was the only way to preserve her strength for her country.

One of her most constant week-end guests—Major-General Bull-Mastiffe, now procured her a job as his driver, and after a week's delay—while she was waiting for her own tailor to make her uniform—she took up her new work, and for six months carried on these useful though onerous duties, until an unfortunate misunderstanding lost the War Office one of their most tireless and skilled employees. One evening the General asked Mipsie to drive his Adjutant, Captain Quickly, to a training camp in Lincolnshire called Skindale. My sister, with pardonable ignorance, never having heard of the place, motored him to Skindles at Maidenhead instead, and not till they arrived—the evening being very dark—did the Captain find out her mistake. Being landed there somewhat late it seemed only common sense to fortify themselves with dinner, but though they of course went on to Lincolnshire the very next day, the General, unluckily, became most irate with his Adjutant, and almost as angry with poor Mipsie. A coolness sprang up between them, and though my sister did her utmost to bridge it by zealous attention to duty—often cutting short her daily lunches with Captain Quickly in order to be certain of being on time for her boss, it was useless, and in 1940 she was advised to resign.

Soon came the awful time when England, as Mipsie has so often done during her chequered life, stood alone. And after that—the blitz.

Mipsie was always quite fearless in that ordeal. As she said laughingly, she was herself an incendiary bomb at heart, and as for the black-out—'to those who have passed giddy youth and have learnt wisdom, darkness is often a friend,' she once said. She was indeed a child of nature.

She was soon plunged in war work again, for she could never bear to be idle. So in the autumn of 1940 she took on the managership of a Mayfair Beauty Parlour, and helped in the unselfish task of preserving the youth and glamour of those who felt these feminine treasures slipping from them in the stress of the war. It was a fine job to do, all the more so as it was, at first anyway, uphill work. Other well-known rival establishments, staff troubles and shortage of materials were the main worries. She was unable to obtain the right substance for mud packs and so took up a large bin of mud from our sewage farm—unluckily there were one or two tadpoles therein (quite harmless, but customers are so silly). She tried to replace unobtainable henna with Condy's fluid but forgot that it also stains skin, and she lost a rich client of long standing during the ensuing dispute. But the staff was her real headache. As the call-up accelerated it was well-nigh impossible to get skilled assistants, and cleaners were more scarce still. Then suddenly, all her troubles were solved by her own genius.

She was working late one evening, trying to solve her difficulties, so late that almost her only remaining cleaner was already busy, sweeping the pile carpet vigorously. Sub-consciously, as Mipsie noted the lean, energetic figure at work, she could not help comparing her with some of the clients who came to her for slimming treatment and reducing baths. 'How do you keep your figure, Mrs. Meat?' she inquired laughingly. 'Just 'ard work, M'Lady,' came the reply. 'I don't 'ave no time to get fat.'

Instantly the idea flashed through Mipsie's brain. Why not kill two birds with one stone—let her clients clean the *salon* and reduce fat in the process, saving her also the eternal hunt for staff? The scheme was soon put into action and became most popular. The twenty guinea course included the polishing room, where Mrs. Meat would bring all the articles that needed rubbing up each day, sweeping with a stiff brush and an electric sweeper (specially recommended for redundance of flesh round the waist) and finally scrubbing floors—an advanced stage at an advanced cost, for Mipsie found that unless they had to pay more for it the clients would refuse that part of the course altogether. Afterwards came the special facial tone-up, massage and manicure, to put right any damage the treatment had done, and then the client would leave the *salon* a slimmer and a healthier woman. None returned for another course which proves its efficacy.

It was only a step from that to another brilliant scheme. In 1941 Mipsie opened a Cleaners' Agency in Kensington, where for a substantial fee customers could hire out the services of houseworkers. The two businesses were kept entirely separate and were never connected with each other, so it was sheer ill luck that one cleaner should have been inadvertently sent to *clean her own house*. Worse still, on the hall table were two bills; one from the Beauty *salon*, another from the Kensington Agency. She was not very nice about the whole thing and nor were other friends of hers who were also Mipsie's patrons. My sister felt that she could not continue if she did not have her patron's confidence, so she immediately closed the Cleaners' Agency and resigned her managership of the Beauty *salon*.

Another sad chapter in her life was closed.

XXVII

THE REWARD OF MERIT

It is with a full heart that I pen this last chapter of my beautiful sister's life story. For three things have happened to give me cause for great rejoicing and thankfulness. Mipsie was released from jail last week, her sentence having been considerably reduced on account of charming conduct, she has just announced that she is engaged to be married yet again, and I am once more a proud grandmother!

Perhaps I may be forgiven if I refer to my own excitement—which actually happened several weeks ago—first. Those who read my last series in these pages will remember my dear girl Margaret, who wedded Private—now Lieut., I am thankful to say—Paul White of the West Indian Regiment nearly a year ago. He has proved a good and devoted husband, his poor sight getting decidedly worse, which is a blessing in many directions, one of the ways being that he hopes to get demobilized quite soon, when they will all live at Little Bengers Farm and Paul will help Addle with his pigs, which he can see quite well with his strongest glasses. I shall thus have my dear girl and little grandson for daily companions.

John Hirsute McClutch White—Addle insisted on his being named after him—is doubly dear to me because he is already the living image, both in looks and character, of his great-aunt Mipsie. He refuses to take his bottle unless he has a bright jewel on a ribbon swinging to and fro in front of him, and Addle, who adores his new grandchild, sat last week for over an hour on Nannie's day off, while Margaret was going over some linen with me (they are staying at Bengers) holding his pearl tie-pin so that little Hirsie could suck the end. He dared not let go in case the child injured himself with the sharp point and the moment he took the pin away baby roared. How we laughed when we returned to the nursery! It might have been Mipsie in that cradle.

But to return to the real Mipsie. My dear readers will remember the terrible tragedy that overtook her last summer in consequence of her activities in The Alert, a Firewatchers' Dance Club which she started in 1943 in a blitzed Mayfair cellar. In all innocence, anxious only to do the best for her men-folk, like any true woman (none of this dreadful equality of sexes for her; her whole life, she has often said, has been based on the difference between them) she bought rashly perhaps, and too trustingly from unwise sources. What did a word like 'black market' mean to her, who has never looked on the black side of anything? So she suffered for her ignorance, as others have before her. To our horror we learnt suddenly that she had been arrested, and subsequently she was condemned to twelve months in the second division. What an insult, not even to put a British aristocrat in the first division!

All through that dreadful time I have been her most constant visitor, and indeed have compiled this biography with the aid of the notes which she prepared for me. She has been the old gay, gallant Mipsie in spite of it all, though she has felt the privations, especially the lack of cocktails, cigarettes and man-power, most terribly I know. Yet even within those bare walls romance can bloom, as my readers will hear.

One of her kindest and most regular visitors was the prison chaplain, who also lent her his rubber hot-water

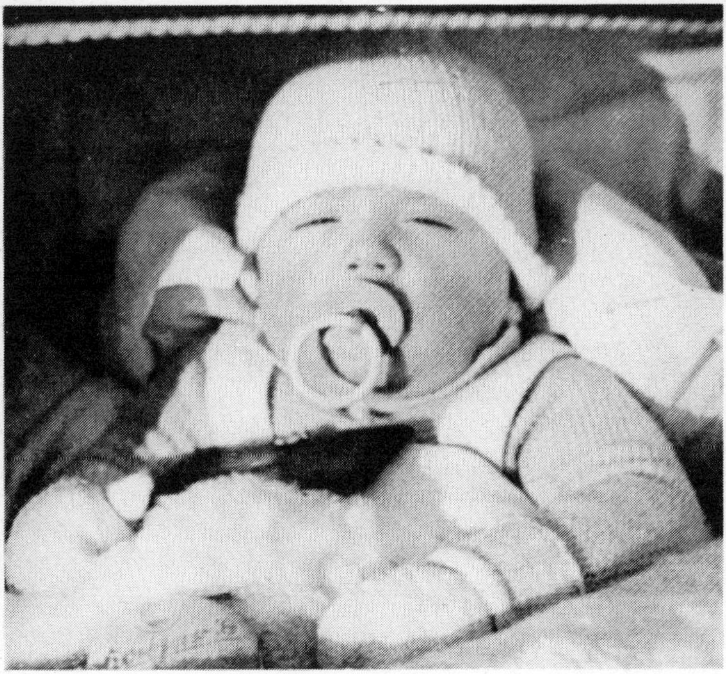

LITTLE HIRSIE

bottle—the act of a very '*parfait knight*' indeed. He talked much to Mipsie of her past life and made her realize that she had, possibly, made mistakes which she would fain undo. Was it too late to turn over a new leaf? Mipsie, in the quiet of her cosy little cell, pondered long over the words and the character of her new friend. She began to realize that perhaps the love of a good man is better than titles and a homely hot-water bottle more precious than rubies. Then suddenly—in the still watches of one night, a strange thing happened. The worn rubber bottle split! And as the warm water flowed over my sister's feet and legs there flowed also over her heart the conviction that she was no fit wife for a clergyman. Henceforth she was friendly to the chaplain but not encouraging.

When the day came for her to leave she said good-bye to many with regret—her wardress, who gave her a parting present of all her clothing coupons, her fellow-prisoners, many of whom were serving sentences for the same mistakes that Mipsie had made, and above all the Governor—Colonel Sir Augustus (Gusto) Royster, an old soldier with a past record of gallantry and daring and a present reputation of mellowed kindness and good sportsmanship which made him popular with all. As Mipsie took his hand she found there were tears in her eyes. 'I have never been so happy as under your care,' she said. 'Please come up and see me some time.' (I don't know why she said 'come up,' for the sitting-rooms of her little Mayfair house are on the ground floor.)

Well, my dear, dear readers can guess the rest. The Governor took her at her word next day. He took her out to dinner the following evening. Mipsie learnt that he was a widower, with a charming little place near Newmarket and some good shooting in Scotland. Within a week they were engaged, and mean to be married as soon as Gusto can resign from the governorship of the prison. Mipsie tried to dissuade him from this course, fearing that he would miss the interest of his work (as well as the salary), but he replied very gallantly that he would not need any more criminals to look after now that he had Mipsie. They will not be rich, I fear. But my dear sister, with touching humility, says that she has learnt much from her fellow-prisoners which will enable her, in spite of rations and shortages, to live with her new husband in a manner befitting the rank and beauty of, I feel confident that every reader will agree with me, one of the most remarkable women of our time.

Lady Addle Remembers
Ed: Mary Dunn

Lady Addle Remembers: being the delicious, pompous, outrageous and gloriously funny memoirs of Lady Blanche Addle of Eigg (nee Coot of Coot's Balder).

Lady Addle, when asked, nay begged, to write her memoirs, at first hesitated. She had played halma with Lord Salisbury, knitted a comforter for the king, bicycled with Bismarck. It was not fitting, she thought, to write of such intimate moments. But finally, conceding that it was her duty to England, she consented to reveal All.

Here are her memories of childhood at Coot's Balder, her whirlwind romance of only three years followed by the Wedding of the Year to John Hector Murdoch Hirsute McClutch, 17th Baron of Eigg (bridesmaids wore dresses of tartan serge with chip hats trimmed with thistles), and the story of her sister, dear brave Mipsie, who underwent such tragedy and sorrow that in middle age her hair turned chestnut in a single night.

'A brilliant and hilarious parody of Victorian memoirs . . . highly recommended'
CHRISTOPHER SIMON SYKES

'I strongly recommend readers to share Lady Addle's recollections'
TIMES LITERARY SUPPLEMENT

'A first rate spoof'
HUGO VICKERS

'Brilliantly funny photographs'
NICHOLAS COLERIDGE

'Lady Addle is *essential*'
COUNTRY LIFE

0 552 99191 0 £2.50

BLACK SWAN

Lady Addle at Home

Ed: Mary Dunn

Blanche, Lady Addle's contribution to the Home Front in the last war is just as appropriate in these days of austerity. In this volume she reveals some of those delightful home-maker secrets which are prized by economy-minded hostesses all over the world!

How to make Bisque d'Horreur. Use only the best rat-stock — being careful to skin your rat first.

A Cure for Sleeplessness. Take a large Spanish onion to bed with you. You will have such a bad night that the following one you will find that nothing will keep you awake.

A Good Substitute for a Sun Tan. Mix ammonia with brown boot polish. Rub up with an old sock.

The Colour of Fish. This should be bright and clear. Remove the fishmonger's fingermarks with a little arsenic and polish with old lace.

Plus! How to make goat's milk go further! Cures for bags under the eyes! How to build up the physique of your goldfish!
AND HUNDREDS MORE!

What the critics said about *Lady Addle Remembers:*

'Consistently funny'
MARY ANNE BONNEY, PUNCH

'Will give pleasure to many'
ISABEL COLEGATE, SPECTATOR

'Hilarious parody . . . highly recommended'
CHRISTOPHER SIMON-SYKES

'So delicate, so subtle . . . real delight'
ANGELA HUTH, LISTENER

0 552 99235 6

£2.50

BLACK SWAN

The Eliza Stories

by Barry Pain

'I was brought up on the Eliza books and treasure them greatly. They provide a laugh a minute'
ARTHUR MARSHALL

The first book about Eliza and her dreadful husband appeared in 1900, and over the next twelve years the popularity of this suburban couple encouraged their author to produce further volumes, all five of which are included in *The Eliza Stories*.

Described by Terry Jones as 'some of the funniest stories in the English language,' they tell the tale of Eliza and her husband (who is never named) through everyday incidents, all told with priggish and pompous exactitude by the husband — a comic character at whose gullibility and foolishness we can only laugh, and secretly sympathise — recognising in him the human weaknesses we all share.

The Eliza Stories are as fresh and funny today as the day they were written.

'I am delighted that a new edition of the Eliza stories has been published. I have been having my own dog-eared copies read aloud to me, which is the best test, and I find them as amusing as I did fifty years ago.'
JOHN BETJEMAN

'Not to be missed . . . very funny'
GEOFFREY LEE, COUNTRY LIFE

'Anybody who can read *The Eliza Stories* without considerable amusement and pleasure would have to be a very dull creature'
MIRANDA SEYMOUR, BOOKS & BOOKMEN

0 552 99190 2 £3.95

BLACK SWAN

Mrs. Pooter's Diary
Keith Waterhouse

'The whole book is a bundle of fun . . . it is ingenious and it is immensely entertaining'
DAILY MAIL

"The Laurels"
Brickfield Terrace
Holloway.

I have discovered (although he does not yet know that I know!) what it is that my husband does in the quarter-of-an-hour before retiring each night. If he may entertain hopes of publishing a diary, then so may I – after all, it is not as if my dear Charlie were a 'Somebody' whose thoughts and impressions are any more profound or worthwhile than the next person's. He is, alas, thanks to the good nature that holds him back, no more of a 'Somebody' than is –
Mrs. Charles Pooter

The Diary of a Nobody is one of the great classics of English humour. *Mrs. Pooter's Diary* is more than a brilliant homage to the original, it is a wonderful comic creation in its own right.

'Mr. Waterhouse does it brilliantly . . . had me in stitches'
AUBERON WAUGH, DAILY MAIL

'What Waterhouse has managed is to re-create the whole Pooter world, as if in a three-dimensional model, and then show it to us from a quite different pespective . . . Most readers like the Pooters, and I suspect quite a few of us admire them and even envy them; Waterhouse has left that affection intact'
SIMON HOGGART, OBSERVER

0 552 99117 1 £3.95

BLACK SWAN

Queen Lucia

E. F. Benson

'We will pay anything for Lucia books'

NOEL COWARD: GERTRUDE LAWRENCE: NANCY MITFORD: W. H. AUDEN

Queen Lucia is set in the middle-class, garden-party world of the 1920's, a society dominated utterly and ruthlessly by the greatest arch-snob who has ever existed. Lucia and her cohorts – Georgie with his dyed hair, embroidery, and piano duets, Daisy Quantock with her passion for the new and exotic – capture the mood and flavour of a whole period, and the nuances and rivalries of English life are described engrossingly and with a rapier wit.

If the pens of Evelyn Waugh and Jane Austen had mated, Lucia would have been the offspring.

'At long last, here she is again, the splendid creature, the great, the wonderful Lucia'
NANCY MITFORD

'My greatest reading pleasure in 1967 was the discovery of E. F. Benson's 'Lucia' novels . . . I enjoyed them so much that I borrowed (and was tempted to steal) two more of the series: and I confess myself a Lucia addict'
TERENCE DE VERE WHITE

'To describe her as a snob would be to describe Leonardo as a talented man'
MICHAEL MACLIAMMOR

0 552 99075 2 £2.95

BLACK SWAN

Lucia in London

E. F. Benson

Lucia, Queen of provincial society, now launches herself onto the London scene. The creme de la creme of social climbers, Lucia never falters as she dons her real (seed) pearls and prepares to attach the beau monde, wheedling her way into parties where she has not been invited and coaxing the rich and titled to come to tea.

Lucia in London is the second of the famous Lucia books by E. F. Benson. Comic masterpieces, these novels of manners are brought to life by sharp, satirical social observations and are as deliciously funny today as they were when first published in the 1920's.

'He was a master of a certain kind of light fiction, and he can delight even though one knows that his satire is ultimately friendly . . . He is clever and funny, but he writes for his victims'
THE SPECTATOR

'The flow of his comic inspiration never dwindles'
ELIZABETH HARVEY

'Here she is again, the splendid creature, the great, the wonderful Lucia . . . I must say I reopened these magic books after some thirty years with misgivings: I feared that they would have worn badly and seem dated. Not at all; they are as fresh as paint. The characters are real and therefore timeless'
NANCY MITFORD

0 552 99076 0 £3.95

BLACK SWAN

Miss Mapp

E. F. Benson

'The flow of his comic inspiration never dwindles'
ELIZABETH HARVEY

Here is the redoubtable 'triumphantly arch of all arch villainesses', Miss Elizabeth Mapp of Tilling — a schemer, a woman of fine habits and low cunning who spends her days in the delightful bow window of her delightful period house, light opera glasses in hand, noting and annotating the business of her neighbours. Not a thing escapes her gimlet eyes, from the purchase of a basket of over-ripe red-currants, to the unfortunate drinking habits of Captain Puffin.

Miss Mapp is the third in the sequence of the famous Lucia novels. Deliciously funny, outrageously U, quintessentially English, Benson's comic characters have come alive again for another generation.

'He was a master of a certain kind of light fiction, and he can delight even though one knows that his satire is ultimately friendly . . . He is clever and funny, but he writes for his victims'
THE SPECTATOR

'My greatest reading pleasure in 1967 was the discovery of E. F. Benson's "Lucia" novels . . . I enjoyed them so much that I borrowed (and was tempted to steal) two more of the series. I confess myself a Lucia addict'
TERENCE DE VERE WHITE

0 552 99083 3 £2.95

BLACK SWAN

Mapp and Lucia
E. F. Benson

'I have not laughed so much at any novel as *Mapp and Lucia* since I read the early Waughs'
TERENCE DE VERE WHITE

At last they meet — the two most formidable ladies in English literature collide in genteel and deadly enmity. Lucia, now widowed, shakes the dust of Riseholme from her elegant feet and, with Georgie Pillson as devoted courtier, prepares to conquer the high society of Tilling. She brings her musical evenings, her Italian, her poetry, and her ambitious snobbery. And Miss Mapp, her features corrugated by chronic rage and curiosity, can only prepare to defend her position as doyenne of Tilling. The town is split in an exciting and scintillating war of garden parties, bridge evenings, and staggeringly simple little dinners.

Mapp and Lucia is the fourth of the Lucia novels, a chronicle of life in two English country towns described with malicious delicacy and wit.

'I might have gone to my grave without ever knowing about Lucia or Miss Mapp. It is not a risk anyone should take lightly'
AUBERON WAUGH

0 552 99084 1 £2.95

BLACK SWAN